Conch Shell Murder

Also by Dorothy Francis
in Large Print:

The Legacy of Merton Manor
Murder in Hawaii
Nurse Under Fire
A Blue Ribbon for Marni
Keys to Love

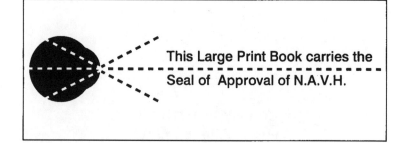

This Large Print Book carries the
Seal of Approval of N.A.V.H.

Conch Shell Murder

Dorothy Francis

WHEELER
PUBLISHING

Published in 2004 by arrangement with
Tekno Books and Ed Gorman.

Wheeler Large Print Cozy Mystery.

The text of this Large Print edition is unabridged.
Other aspects of the book may vary from the original edition.

Set in 16 pt. Plantin.

Printed in the United States on permanent paper.

Library of Congress Cataloging-in-Publication Data

Francis, Dorothy Brenner.
    Conch shell murder / Dorothy Francis.
       p. cm.
    ISBN 1-58724-621-X (lg. print : sc : alk. paper)
    1. Women private investigators — Florida — Key West —
Fiction.   2. Inheritance and succession — Fiction.   3. Key
West (Fla.) — Fiction.   4. Large type books.   I. Title.
PS3556.R327C6 2004
813'.54—dc22
                                             2003070536

For Richard, Ann, and Pat

As the Founder/CEO of NAVH, the only national health agency solely devoted to those who, although not totally blind, have an eye disease which could lead to serious visual impairment, I am pleased to recognize Thorndike Press* as one of the leading publishers in the large print field.

Founded in 1954 in San Francisco to prepare large print textbooks for partially seeing children, NAVH became the pioneer and standard setting agency in the preparation of large type.

Today, those publishers who meet our standards carry the prestigious "Seal of Approval" indicating high quality large print. We are delighted that Thorndike Press is one of the publishers whose titles meet these standards. We are also pleased to recognize the significant contribution Thorndike Press is making in this important and growing field.

Lorraine H. Marchi, L.H.D.
Founder/CEO
NAVH

* Thorndike Press encompasses the following imprints: Thorndike, Wheeler, Walker and Large Print Press.

Prologue

The sleeve of Alexa Chitting's black caftan caught on the conch shell sitting on her polished desk, but she shook it free and crossed the white carpeting of the third-floor office at Chitting Marina like a dowager queen balancing a crown on her sable hair. Her nails gleamed scarlet against the satin drapery she pushed aside in order to see into the January night, where murky moonlight honed masts and riggings into black skeletons.

At her orders, her office had been carpeted and soundproofed against the roar of motors, the cry of dockmasters, the babble of wealthy seafarers on the move. But tonight, Alexa fought a feeling of foreboding, sensed something disconcerting in the silence as her gaze probed the rows of sleek sailing vessels and motor yachts rocking in their slips.

When she heard footsteps grate against the pine of the balcony outside her door, she called out, "Who's there?"

She bristled, well aware of her autocratic tone. All the dockmasters respected her predilection for privacy when she worked late. All had orders never to disturb her. Could there be an emergency? Her cavalier attitude softened a bit. Tyler? Po? It didn't surprise her that she thought of her lover before her husband. She doubted it would have surprised Po, either. Or Tyler.

"Who is it?" She moved from the window to the door. Nobody replied. How dare this intruder ignore her!

Her breath snagged in her throat as she peered through the peephole, seeing a yellow and black wasp-shaped hood, which hid the face of someone wearing a dockmaster's uniform. The black sweatshirt bore the familiar white-lettered words CHITTING MARINA Key West. White pants gleamed in the moonlight filtering between the wrought-iron balcony rails. Alexa screamed as she turned and ran toward her desk phone. Before she could grasp the receiver and dial Marina Security, a key clicked in the lock and the door opened, admitting a chilling blast of sea air along with the sound of waves lapping against boat hulls. Then the door closed.

"Stop!" The command was a muffled hiss. "Don't move."

What sort of an intrusion was this! Thrusting her chin up, Alexa steeled herself to keep in control. She turned to face the intruder, but her voice quavered as she looked at the gun held in a black-gloved hand.

"Who are you? What do you want?" Fright left a bitterness at the base of her tongue.

"Money. Open the safe."

The intruder spoke in a frog-like croak, and Alexa could discern neither sex nor ethnicity. Taking a chance, she reached for the telephone, but her captor pounced on the instrument, jerking the wire from the wall without lowering the gun.

"Open the safe or you die. It's the will-o-the-wasp. Do it!"

"There's no money here. A courier takes all cash to the bank at five."

"Open the safe."

Was this a Chitting employee? Or had a thief stolen a master key from the dockmaster's office? Through the holes in the wasp mask she saw dark eyes blazing like lasers.

"Move!" A nudge with the gun barrel enforced the command.

Hairs at her nape rose as she faced the wall safe, reached for the knob with shaking fingers. The cold steel turned smoothly and easily, and she heard the tumblers fall into place. The door opened.

"Hand over the cash."

A robber! How could she be at the mercy of this unsavory person! An addict needing a fix? The Keys abounded with them. Crack cocaine made users both desperate and dangerous. Where had this one procured the uniform? She would check the supply department tomorrow. Deftly she pulled out a small bundle of bills secured with a red rubber band, hoping her foe wouldn't find the fat envelope of cash she had shoved to the back of the green felt compartment.

"Give it to me."

She noticed a slight tremble in the intruder's gun hand. He was scared — unsure. Maybe she could overpower him. Why should she acquiesce to a hophead! She extended the packet of bills, but when the thief reached out, she dropped it and chopped at his wrist. The gun flew through the air, then thudded onto the carpet.

They both made a dive for the gun. Alexa's perspiring fingers clutched the cold barrel, but her grip slipped. She felt the pistol wrested from her grasp. In seconds the intruder would again be in control. Seizing the fleeting chance for escape, she jumped up, ignored the ripping of her caftan as she stepped on its hem, and rushed into the bathroom, slamming and locking the door.

"Now get out of here! Take the money and go."

The thief pounded on the door. "Open up!"

Alexa sucked in air, her heart pounding. The thief had the money. The phone was out. He knew she couldn't identify him. Why didn't he go? She cowered beside the toilet, waiting for a shot to shatter the fragile door lock. Was he a rapist?

No shot came. Instead she heard a scraping and saw the door handle move. He was using a plastic card to spring the lock. She still cowered by the toilet on aching knees when the door opened.

"Get up or you're dead!"

The threat reverberated against her eardrums, and as she tried to pull herself to her feet, once again she saw the gun hand tremble. What if the gun fired accidentally? She'd been a fool to take a stand. The few dollars lost meant nothing to her. Only in the dark recesses of her mind did she admit that the gunman wanted more than money.

"Go to your desk and sit down."

Gripping the cold porcelain of the toilet, she heaved herself to her feet and limped toward her leather-padded swivel chair. She felt all of her sixty years. Why wasn't this person leaving? He had his money. Or was it a she who had her money? She still couldn't be sure. She sat at her desk, gasping as the intruder raised the gun.

"Wait! What are you doing?" Alexa braced her palms on her desk blotter, trying to help herself stand.

"I'm going to kill you."

"But why?" Her voice escalated with fear. "You've got money for the crack house. Take it and go. Better a robbery rap than a murder rap. Think of the consequences, you fool!"

The thief raised the gun, pulled the trigger, but the shot went wild. Alexa turned, seeing

11

the faint outline of a bullet hole in the corner of the Oriental carpet hanging on the wall behind her desk. The man was crazed. As if by reflex, Alexa grabbed the conch shell on her desk, hurled it at the gun. Smart move. The gun clattered against the desktop. She wanted to snatch it up, but her body ignored her mental command. She could only stare as fear immobilized her.

This time the intruder knocked the gun from her reach and grabbed the conch shell. He eyed its pink and coral spiral for a moment, then stepped behind her desk. With the heel of his hand, he shoved on her chest, slamming her into her chair.

"Take your money and go," Alexa whimpered, hating being forced to beg for anything — even her life. Begging had never been the Chitting style. She tried to divert her attacker's attention by telling him about the money still inside the safe. But it was too late.

With fingers curled inside the conch and thumb gripping one end, the thief slammed the shell's protrusions against Alexa's temple and forehead. She felt blood trickle into her eyes, her mouth, and as a rusty taste coated her tongue, she saw her desk blotter flecked with red stains that quickly darkened to brown. Excruciating pain exploded in her head, expanding from a central core and radiating in all directions. She raised her hands to protect herself, but the blows rained faster and harder until all fight left her.

She slumped, her head a pulpy melon dangling wetly over the chair arm and dripping blood onto the pristine carpet.

Chapter One

Gloom shrouded Key West, and Katie Hassworth shivered in the dusky twilight as she turned her old Ford convertible onto South Roosevelt Boulevard, passing the remains of Houseboat Row and heading toward the McCartel and Hassworth Detective Agency on Simonton Street. The sky was an inverted gray bowl. A January gale mixed fallen palm fronds, torn newspapers, and fast-food cartons like a malevolent salad, tossing them across the narrow spit of island from the Gulf to the Atlantic.

Home. In spite of the nasty weather, she was glad to be back. Slowing her speed, she imagined she could taste salt along with the grit blowing in the air.

"Move it along, lady," a porky teenager shouted from the hood of a speeding purple van bearing the logo CRUISE HOG. "Get that heap going or you'll get run over and miss the parade!"

Kids. Katie ignored the caveat, slowing even more. After two years of island living, Key West seemed more like home than the orphanage where she had spent eighteen years, or the college dorm where she had lived the ten semesters it had taken her to earn a master's degree. It even seemed more like home than the close-to-the-school cottage she had rented while she taught English for five years in Miami.

She was so glad to be back from her Tampa business/pleasure trip that she took the scenic route to Simonton Street, watching the agitated ocean on her left as the wind churned the gray-green waves and wet down the gulls huddled on the low seawall. She passed East Martello Gallery, the airport, posh motels, which on a more pleasant day would have been palm-shaded from the late afternoon sun.

Although it was after five o'clock and she knew most of the action would be at Mallory Dock on the other side of the island where tourists congregated, hoping for a sunset, she drove slowly toward Smathers Beach. In the distance clouds closed in on a gray merchant ship, and she could count three schooners and a shrimper anchored closer to shore.

"Hey, Blondie! How about a lift?"

In an ordinary car she could have been impervious to the call. A convertible made one vulnerable. Not only was it a crazy kind of car to risk one's life in on the overseas highway, but it also allowed one to hear exhortations one might otherwise miss. She pulled over, conscious of traffic whizzing by. Seizing the chance, she stretched her slim

15

legs, kicked off her shoes. Sometimes nothing felt better than kicking off her shoes.

"Where to, Bubba?" she asked as a thin jeans-clad man, shoeless and wearing a gold necklace and a gold stud in his left earlobe, opened the passenger door and slid into the seat.

"Duval." Bubba sniffed as he tucked a long strand of oily black hair behind his right ear. "One of the buskers is reading tarot cards at Duval and Angela, Blondie. Got to see where my fortune lays."

"Lies."

"No lies. Tarot cards speak true. Got to see where my fortune lays."

Katie smiled, knowing she should have ignored the solecism. No use trying to explain the finer points of the language to Bubba, and no point in asking him to refrain from calling her Blondie. He had nicknames for everyone, and many of them were fitting. She gunned the Ford into a short break in the traffic.

"Your fortune might lie in steady employment." She had known Bubba for a year. He odd-jobbed around town, and now and then he supplied her and Mac with valuable information gleaned from the street. He had no qualms about pocketing their money.

"A steady job would cut into my prime time, Blondie. No way."

Katie laughed. "Anything go down while I've been away?"

"Naw. Some old biddy got bumped off last Monday, but I can't recollect her name. Robbery, the police say. It's already fallen out of the news because the buskerfest's been the big deal this week. You seen any of the acts?"

"I've been away."

"The celebration ends tonight with a street parade and a dance. Should be a blast. Got street performers here from sixteen states and five foreign countries." Bubba sniffled and wiped his nose on his shirt sleeve. "The tarot reader's from Germany."

"I'm looking forward to seeing the parade. Sure you can't recall the name of the murder victim?"

"Naw. But for a certain consideration I could look into it for you." He peeked at her from the sides of his eyes.

"Not this time, Bubba." She disliked dealing with a druggie. It wounded her sense of justice. Any help gleaned from Bubba was pure serendipity, and seriously depending on him for assistance would be like hanging paper moons. She drove a few blocks out of her way to let him off near a motley throng on Duval Street, then she returned to her office on Simonton.

Leaving the convertible, Katie strolled to the center of a bricked patio and stooped to dampen a tissue in a small gurgling fountain shaded by a sea grape, an apricot sapling, and a Christmas palm. Retreating a few

17

steps, she polished a salty scum that collected nightly from the gold and black sign that hung on the white picket fence. McCartel and Hassworth. Private Investigators. The fence also supported three bougainvilleas whose wind-damaged blossoms now lay on the old paving brick like drops of pale blood. Even at that, Katie thought the office looked a lot more inviting on the exterior than it did on the interior.

She snapped on the dim hall light inside the white frame building that had once been a small residence. The pine-planked floor slanted toward the rear door, and she wrinkled her nose at the smell of stale cigarette smoke that had penetrated the dingy jute draperies. A glance at the closed doors to the two rear rooms where Mac lived told her he wasn't there, but she looked into his office to make sure before going to her own desk.

They shared the two front rooms as office space, where they each had a battered oak desk and a captain's chair, a typewriter, and a steel filing cabinet. A straight-backed chair for clients sat beside each desk.

"Austere. There's no other word for it." Katie unlocked the bottom file drawer, checking to see that her gun was still there. She hated guns. Only at Mac's insistence did she own one, and its residence in the file drawer served to chronicle her hate.

The light from the hallway streamed into

the room and she opened her center desk drawer. Pulling out a bag of mints, she began nibbling. Her stomach growled. Maybe the sweets would dull her appetite. She quashed that idea and promised herself to eat a nutritious meal that night. She wasn't fat, but she felt fat and she hated the feeling. Frequently, inner fears compelled her to look in a mirror to reassure her that she was still tall and willowy. Maybe it was her round face that made her think fat. Anorectic. Miami doctors had helped her put that scene behind her and she was determined to keep it there.

Just as she was reaching to turn on her desk lamp, the telephone rang.

"McCartel and Hassworth. Katie Hassworth speaking."

"Glad you're back, Katie-girl. Been trying to get you since noon."

"Mac! Good to hear from you. Where are you?" Katie relaxed in her chair, welcoming his sonorous voice.

"Tallahassee. Be here until a week from Monday."

"That long?"

"The Gillian case requires lots of perusal into real estate transactions. With luck I may be able to cut some of the red tape. You can manage the office while I'm away, can't you?"

"Sure, Mac." She spoke with more confidence that she felt. "Anything new on tap?"

19

"No. The report to John Lowery is due on Wednesday, and see if you can collect some of the bills, okay?"

"Right." Katie sighed. Collecting the bills frequently burgeoned into a big problem. "Got a number where I can reach you?"

Mac gave her his motel number, talked a bit more, then signed off.

Disappointment at knowing she wouldn't see Mac for over a week made her reach for another mint. No romance linked them, but at the forensic session in Tampa, many of the unusual terms and techniques she had heard discussed were beyond her comprehension. She needed Mac to explain them, to bolster her confidence in herself as a detective. They had worked together for two years, but she had only earned her P.I. license and been bonded a few months ago. She hoped nothing big would come up in the next ten days.

The room grew dark as night fell, but instead of turning on the lamp, she closed the door, blocking out the glow from the hallway. Sometimes she still felt as if she were play acting as a detective and if she turned on a bright light, her job might vanish and she'd find herself — where?

She'd come a long ways from that orphanage where nobody really cared about her. It had been years since she had bothered to wonder why her parents abandoned her. She also tried to avoid thinking about her marriage to David and the excruciatingly painful divorce when he found "someone else." That was when the anorexia started. She sighed.

After five years of teaching English in a Miami middle school, she thought she had put David behind her. She thought she had arrived. But just when she began eating normally again and could think of David without an emotional upheaval, Jon McCartel brought a gun to class. He shot and killed another student before turning the weapon on her and then on himself.

That had ended her teaching career. The experience shattered her confidence, transformed her in a way that allowed no turning back. For weeks nightmares traumatized her, replaying the terrorizing moments on the screen of her mind. For months a fog of guilt added to her sense of failure. Why hadn't she realized that Jon was homicidal and suicidal? She found no satisfactory answers.

She recovered from her bullet wound, but she finished out the school year on sick leave. Mac McCartel, Jon's father, resigned from the Miami police force, and she helped him find his son's drug supplier and bring him to justice. His incarceration had given them both satisfaction.

Mac wanted to forget everything about Miami. And so did she. When he invited her to work with him in opening a private detective agency in Key West, she said yes, knowing that many of their cases would be drug related. Maybe she had taken the line of least resistance. She preferred to think she was evening a score for Jon McCartel, but in spite of that, she sometimes still felt guilty at abandoning her teaching career.

Outside, someone sounded a woeful blast on a conch shell, snapping Katie from her reverie. She reached for another mint, then locked the office and headed for the buskerfest parade.

Chapter Two

Darkness fell quickly in the Keys once the sun had set, and Katie locked her car door before she set out on foot, lowering her head into the wind as she walked down Simonton toward Front Street. No point in taking wheels. There would be no parking place unless she pulled into her own driveway. Some tourist eager to see the busker parade might have encroached upon even that small spot.

Now she wished she had gone home first, showered, changed into fresh clothes, stopped at Loguns for a meal. Her third-floor apartment in Diane Dade's old Victorian mansion was only a few blocks away, but the flow of the crowd carried her toward the parade route.

"Hot dogs! Get your hot dogs here!"

The stentorian cry of the Front Street vendor along with the smell of grilled pork pulled her in that direction. Food. Hardly a balanced meal, but she promised herself to pick up some fruit and milk later. She would have to grocery shop first thing tomorrow.

"One please." She paid for the hot dog then added copious portions of mustard, pickles, onions. Standing on a low retaining wall to view the parade scene, she savored the saltiness of the meat, the tartness of the toppings, as she tried to keep mustard from dripping on her shirt.

The street performers were an anachronistic mix — like visitors straight from the Middle Ages, straight from some wealthy lord's castle where they had crossed the drawbridge and performed in exchange for roast boar, wine, and a night's lodging.

The juggler in the hot pink leotard tossed five oranges in the air as he pranced to a Highland tune played by a kilted bagpiper strong on the drone bass. With his hands gripping his ankles, a contortionist wearing an electric blue bikini walked along, grinning at the crowd from between his knees.

"Ladies and gentlemen — The Great Gorinni!" A sword swallower stopped long enough to ease a flashing steel blade down his gullet, remove it, and bow to his audience.

"The Great Gorinni, ladies and gentlemen, and you saw him at the buskerfest parade."

Garbed like a skeleton, the tarot card reader walked beside a man who had draped his shoulders and arms with iguanas and what Katie hoped were non-poisonous snakes. She felt like a cliché as she shuddered. Why did snakes bring out such fear in people!

"Katie! When did you get back?"

Looking in the direction of the familiar voice, Katie smiled as she saw Diane threading her way toward her. Diane had that effect on everyone. People automatically smiled at her. Her denim wrap-around skirt emphasized both her plumpness and her short stature, but her wedge-cut brown hair, sky-blue eyes, and oval face held one's attention. Usually Diane exuded an enviable contentment, but tonight her face looked pinched and the corners of her mouth drooped.

"How's the happy homemaker?" Katie teased gently. Diane was a feminist, but her career choice centered on home and family. It surprised Katie to see her without Randy and their two kids.

"Why didn't you stop by the house?" Diane asked when she reached Katie's side.

"I just got in town so thought I should check in at the office first. Then I got caught up in the parade." She stopped talking when she noticed Diane's strained expression hadn't eased. "Something's wrong?"

Diane gripped Katie's elbow, guiding her to the edge of the throng. "I've been hoping you'd get home soon. I need to talk to you — about Mother. You haven't heard?"

Katie shook her head, sensing bad news to come as she followed Diane, the parade forgotten.

"She's dead, Katie. Murdered. Last Monday

25

night." Diane's voice sounded distraught, but not tearful, and Katie reached for her hand.

Some old biddy got bumped off last Monday. Alexa Chitting. She should have pressed Bubba for more details.

"I'm sorry, Diane. So very sorry." She squeezed Diane's hand as she looked into her eyes. "Who . . . why didn't you let me know? Why didn't you call? You had my emergency number. Why didn't . . ."

"Your first vacation in two years," Diane said. "I wasn't going to spoil it. But I did talk to your partner."

"And?" Katie thought it strange Mac had left no message about the murder. Nor had he mentioned it in their brief phone conversation. Alexa and Porter Chitting were prominent and wealthy citizens of Key West.

"McCartel said he felt that the police were handling the case adequately."

Katie heard Diane's note of bitterness, or perhaps it was despair. "Listen, let's go home. I want you to tell me all about it, but not here on the street." She knew Diane and her mother had been estranged in recent years, but . . .

"Good evening, ladies."

"Mayor Layton!" Diane forced brightness into her voice as she called above the sound of the wind. "Nice to see you."

Katie wished she felt less wary. Why did Rex Layton seem to be turning up in her life

26

so often lately? She sensed a planned casualness that bothered her, but maybe she was wrong. Perhaps it was Diane who had caught Rex's attention. Diane served on several civic committees. A mayor would do well to have Diane on his side of an issue.

Rex Layton towered over Katie by several inches, and the mid-thirties had added pounds to his rangy frame that flattered and gave him the appearance of stability. Eyeing his white slacks and red sports shirt that the wind was pasting to his body, Katie thought mayors shouldn't look so tanned and handsome. Nor should they drive Corvettes. It bothered her that she noticed such a multiplicity of details about him.

"Enjoying the parade?" Diane asked Rex when Katie seemed tongue-tied.

"Buskers and buskerfests have never been my big thing, but the tourists seem charmed." Rex's hazel eyes flashed and he ran his strong fingers through his thick brown hair.

"I find the buskers interesting," Diane said. "Up to a point."

"To each his own." Rex slapped his car keys against his palm. "I was just passing by when I saw you two chatting. May I treat you to a cup of Cuban coffee?" He nodded toward a small hole-in-the-wall grocery. "It's out of the wind, and Mama Montez brews the best on the island."

"Thanks, Rex, but not tonight." Katie spoke up quickly, hoping she didn't appear unfriendly as she demurred. "I just arrived back in town a few minutes ago and I'm really bushed."

"And I'll take a rain check, too," Diane said, smiling.

"Another time then." Rex turned to leave, calling over his shoulder, "Enjoy the parade."

"Why are you so perverse?" Diane asked. "I know he has a rakish reputation as a ladies' man, but maybe he just hasn't found the right lady yet. I know a dozen women who'd . . ."

Before Diane could complete her sentence they saw a tall, dark-haired woman approach Rex, turn to link her arm through his in a proprietary manner, and walk on through the crowd with him, gazing into his face as if mesmerized.

"Who's that?" Katie asked.

"Her name's Elizabeth Wright. She's head of the local office of the Department of Community Affairs. Now aren't you sorry you refused that coffee?"

"It's you I want to talk to, Diane. Let's walk the few blocks home. I can get my car later. I want to hear about your mother. Give me the details. When. Where. How. Who."

"It happened last Monday night — almost a week ago now."

"Just after I left town."

"Right. Mother chose to work late at the marina. She was in her third-floor office when an intruder entered and killed her." Diane's voice broke, and Katie remained silent until Diane regained her composure.

"The intruder broke in?" Katie asked.

"There was no sign of forced entry."

"She was shot?"

"No. She was bludgeoned with a conch shell. I can hardly bear . . . to think of it."

"Maybe we should wait until tomorrow to discuss it," Katie said, wondering what sort of person would choose a conch shell as a murder weapon.

"No. No. I'm all right. I want you to hear about it now. Maybe you can help find the killer."

"Aren't the police working on the case?"

"They say they are, but they seem only to see what they want to see. The obvious. The killer took money from Mother's safe. Over five hundred dollars."

"So I suppose the police are calling it a snatch and grab," Katie said.

"What?"

"They're guessing that some druggie grabbed the money to help support his habit and your mother happened to get in his way."

"Right. That's their theory at this point. But it's never been my theory."

"You think your mother had a mortal enemy?"

"I believe that's quite possible. Mother wasn't exactly the Miss Congeniality of the Keys. Many people knew her as a hard-nosed businesswoman who demanded her way about things and who had the money to back up those demands."

"Every community has its hard-nosed businesspeople, and they don't get murdered with conch shells."

"It's no secret that Mother and Tyler Parish were lovers. Their assignations were well known. That miffed some of the city's lovely ladies who envisioned themselves as possible companions of a glamorous artist."

"I can hardly picture a lovely lady murdering with a conch shell."

"But it could be possible. And as president of the Key West Preservation Group, Mother stepped on lots of toes in the business community. She could have had a mortal enemy."

"Who discovered the body?"

"Mary Bethel, Mother's secretary."

"When? A discoverer of bodies is always of special interest to investigators, as is the victim's spouse."

"Mary discovered Mother's body on Tuesday morning when she went to work. It was a terrible shock to her, but she has been most cooperative in the police investigation."

"What are the cops saying now?"

"Not much." Diane snorted. "When they don't have a strong lead on a suspect within the first twenty-four hours after a crime, they say the trail grows very stale."

"That's true. But it's no reason to give up."

"I think they've done just that. Given up. Sometimes I think the druggies are going to decimate the whole state — the nation. How can a police force with minuscule funds fight criminals who can pour billions of dollars into their defense?"

"A good question. But you said you didn't think your mother's death was drug related. Why?" They had reached the Dade mansion, and Diane paused a second at the wide horseshoe drive.

"There are some things I haven't told you yet. Come on inside."

Chapter Three

The Victorian mansion loomed above them, its first- and second-story verandas and gingerbread trim gleaming white in the glow from the street light. On sunny days the house reminded Katie of a grand dame decked out in frills and lace, but tonight in the cold, dank wind, the mansion was more like a mausoleum. Katie felt the cold of the black iron handrail and heard the gray painted steps squeak under their weight as Diane peered through the leaded glass window in the door before opening it and stepping inside. Katie sniffed the ever-present fragrance of lemon oil.

As they closed the door, Randy Dade called to Diane from the kitchen.

"Parade over, Hon? The buskers all back in buskerland?"

"We left early. Katie's here and we need to talk. Where are the kids?"

"In bed sleeping like dead dolphins. Too exhausted to last out the parade." Randy poked his head through the kitchen doorway to greet Katie. "Can I get you a beer?"

Katie thought Randy's sleek, muscled frame seemed at odds with the fragile-looking *boiserie* of the entryway, just as the elegant gold doubloon he wore around his neck seemed at odds with his worn jeans and T-shirt. Before going into business for himself as a backcountry fishing guide, Randy had once worked as a diver for Mel Fisher in his search for the *Atocha*. He still wore his long blond hair secured by a leather thong at his nape, much as he had worn it while diving for the Spanish galleon.

"No beer, thanks," Katie said. "But I might go for a cup of strong tea."

"Gotcha," Randy said.

"Tea," Diane agreed. "Fewer calories. Let's sit in the kitchen."

As Diane led the way through a front parlor decorated in the French style from the Napoleon II era, Katie admired both the furniture and the ornate display of ginger jars and cut glass in the china cabinet. Diane's family rated her first attention, but the house with its turn-of-the-century frills and its antiques showed the effects of her scrupulous attention. She spent hours keeping the mansion and its tropical garden in tip-top shape.

"Have a chair, Katie," Diane said when they reached the kitchen. She laid her purse on the bricked center bar as Randy filled a copper teakettle and set it on a modern stove ensconced on a tiled hearth within the arch that once had housed a much larger wood range.

Randy pulled out chairs for Katie and

Diane, then joined them. "I think we need your help, Katie. But I guess Diane's already hinted at that."

"Yes. But I need more facts about the . . . murder. And I also need to know what Mac McCartel told you. Katie said you talked with him."

"Mac agrees with the police that Alexa was murdered during a robbery. Probably a drug-related robbery. He wasn't interested in the case — said he was leaving for Tallahassee and that he had more work than he could handle right now."

Katie wondered about that. The agency was fairly new. They seldom had so much work that they could afford to turn down more. Intuitively she knew Mac must have believed the police were on top of the Chitting murder.

"Diane said there were more things about the murder that I needed to know. Care to tell me about them?"

"I'll let Diane do that," Randy said. "Hear her out and then see what you think. McCartel could be right. Maybe the police are doing an adequate job. Maybe we really don't need a private detective."

"I think we do." The teakettle whistled and Diane poured boiling water over the tea bags in their cups, serving the drinks when the brew grew dark. "Sugar?"

"No thanks." Katie sipped the hot liquid,

almost burning her tongue. "So what else is there to know about your mother's death?"

"The murderer stole money, Katie, but he also left an envelope of cash in the back of the safe. If robbery was his motive, why didn't he take *all* the money?"

"Maybe he overlooked it."

"Could be, I suppose. But I doubt it. Then there's the murder weapon to consider."

"Right," Randy agreed. "I'm with Diane on that one. Wouldn't a robber go armed with a gun? Surely he wouldn't depend on finding an appropriate weapon at the scene. Of course, with a druggie, you never know what to expect."

"Mother was robust," Diane said. "She had a personal trainer. She also worked out at a gym four times a week. It would have taken a strong person to overpower her."

"Tell me about the conch shell," Katie said. "Where did it come from?"

"Mother always kept it on her desk. Lots of people keep conch shells around for their beauty, but this one was more than a decoration. Mother was a fifth-generation Conch — born and raised in Key West. Her family followed old traditions."

"Meaning?" Katie absently stirred her sugarless tea, waiting for Diane to continue.

"In more bucolic times Key West had no telephones. When a new baby arrived, the family made the announcement by pounding a stick into the ground and suspending a conch shell from it. The conch on Mother's desk had announced her birth. It was special. At least special to her. She loved telling its story to anyone who asked and would listen."

"That's interesting," Katie said. "And to have the birth shell used as a murder weapon in death is ironic."

"We've told the police about the will," Diane said, "but they've made no comment."

"What about the will?" Katie asked. "Who stands to inherit?"

"It depends on which will you're talking about," Randy said.

"There were two wills?"

"Yes," Diane said. "Of course only one is legal, but Mother recently had a new will drawn by her lawyer. She died before she could sign it."

"So who stood to inherit?" Katie asked.

"Tell her the whole story," Randy said. "Start at the beginning."

Diane took a sip of tea, then began. "Mother had recently learned she had cancer. The doctor's prognosis called it terminal. For a while she denied the bad news. Then she flew into scathing tirades of anger. Temper tantrums. The doctor called her reactions normal. Mother hated everyone — especially her family. To vent her anger, she decided to cut everyone from her will and bequeath her entire estate to the Key West Preservation Group."

"But she died before she could sign that will," Katie said. "So that still leaves the question of who will inherit from the original will and how much."

"I think someone might have killed her who didn't want to see his inheritance disappear with the enactment of the new will," Diane said.

"Could be true," Katie agreed. "Do the police know all this?"

"Yes," Diane said. "But if they're taking any action on the knowledge, they're keeping it to themselves. It's easier to suspect a stranger who's disappeared."

"Diane," Katie said, "tell me. Just who does inherit under your mother's present will?"

"All of us. There's Dad and me. The kids. Randy — indirectly, of course. Tyler Parish, Mother's . . . friend. Mary Bethel, her secretary."

"Anyone else?" Katie asked.

"No," Diane said. "That's all."

"Is there anything else I should know about the case?"

Diane and Randy exchanged glances, then Diane spoke. "Yes. There is. The police found a blood-soaked dockmaster's uniform and a wasp-like Halloween mask and head cover near Mother's body."

"And?" Katie sensed more to come.

"As the police were going over Mother's

office, they also found a blood-stained button on the carpet beside her chair."

"Could they identify the owner?" Katie asked.

"Yes." Diane hesitated, took another sip of tea, then looked away. "There's no denying that the button came from Dad's suede sport coat."

"Do the police have any explanation for how the button got there?"

"None that they're sharing with us," Diane said. "So far Dad and I are avoiding the subject. Neither of us has mentioned it. Dad went to Mother's office now and then. He could have lost the button without knowing it."

"Of course that's a possibility," Katie agreed.

"Katie, the problem is that we need someone to really investigate the case and keep us informed as to what's going on. I think the police have put it on hold and I want to see some action. Someone killed my mother and it's wrong for a murderer to walk the streets scot-free."

"Will you take the case?" Randy asked. "I agree with Diane that we need a private detective."

Katie wanted to say yes. How could she refuse this friend who had opened her home to her, who had given her a place to live in a city were decent rentals were almost impossible to find. She liked both Diane and Randy and she agreed with Diane that a murderer should face justice. But she couldn't say yes quite yet.

"Let me think about it, please. Before I can make a commitment, I need to talk with Mac. I'm the ancillary member of the agency, and I usually go along with his decisions."

"Gotcha," Randy said, nodding.

"Will you be able to talk with him tomorrow?" Diane asked.

"Yes. I can let you know tomorrow. But right now it's getting late, and I need to go back to the office for my car and my luggage."

"I'll drive you," Diane offered. "There's a street dance going on, and the crowd may be raucous."

Katie pushed her teacup aside, but before she could rise to leave, someone knocked on the door.

Chapter Four

Randy answered the door and greeted Beck Dixon, the Dades' next-door neighbor. He pushed her into the kitchen like a brig under full sail, but she took one look at Katie and hesitated.

"Dear children, I didn't know you had company. Didn't mean to intrude."

"You're never an intrusion, Beck." Diane pulled up a chair and set out another teacup. "You know Katie."

"Of course." Beck nodded to Katie. "Glad you're back."

Katie guessed Beck to be about sixty, and while her astringent voice sometimes grated, Katie admired her slim figure and her penchant for wearing jumpsuits that accented her height. Beck had designed her suit with a cleverly disguised drop seat and had commissioned the local handprint fabric shop to make it up in seven colors. Tonight she wore a white hibiscus-flowered cotton that matched her red Kino sandals and the scarlet blossom she had tucked into her ash brown hair.

"I'm not company, Beck," Katie said. "You know that. Anyway, I was just leaving."

"Don't go yet," Diane said. "We need to talk some more."

Beck joined them at the snack bar, accepting the tea with a nod of thanks before she turned to Katie. "Have they talked you into taking the case?"

"You knew they were trying to?"

"It was partly my idea," Beck said. "Alexa was my childhood friend, my benefactor, my colleague in the Preservation Group. I want to see her murderer caught and punished. Since you're a detective and living right here, you seem like a logical person to turn to."

"Right," Randy said.

"I'll help you all I can," Beck promised.

"In what way?" Katie asked.

Beck laughed. "Dear child, I read a lot of detective novels. What else does a lonely spinster have to do! Anyway, I know that sleuths need informants. That's me. Old Sponge Ears. I hear things. A body doesn't run a tea room for thirty years without being privy to a few secrets and lots of gossip."

"Detectives have to operate on facts," Katie said, smiling.

Diane freshened Katie's tea. "Beck deals in facts, too, and flotillas of people pass through the Hibiscus House Tea Room in the course of a few days."

"People talk," Beck said. "And I listen. Are you going to take the case?"

"Maybe. My partner's out of town for a

while, and I've never handled a murder case. Maybe if you waited until Mac gets back . . ."

"Wait, wait, wait!" Beck banged her cup down so hard the tea sloshed into the saucer. "There's already been too much waiting. Once a case gets cold it's much harder to solve."

Katie regretted having revealed her lack of confidence in herself. "If the police have no lead within twenty-four hours, they may never get one. I'm not insensate to those statistics."

"That's why we need you," Diane said. "I suspect the case is no longer top priority with the police."

"Got a notebook with you?" Beck asked Katie.

Katie shook her head.

"Thought detectives always carried notebooks. They do on TV." Beck pulled a notebook from her jumpsuit pocket. "Here. Use this." She handed Katie a ballpoint. "What you need to do first is to make a list of suspects."

Katie tried not to smile at Beck's combination of bossiness and child-like enthusiasm. "Okay. Number one. Who'll it be?" She waited, ballpoint poised, eager to hear whose name would be mentioned first.

"Any of the family," Diane said. "You can write my name in the number one slot if you want to, but from a financial standpoint, any of us might have had the motivation to do away with Mother. I told you, we'd all inherit.

42

She didn't simply bequeath everything to Dad."

"Humph!" Beck snorted. "Po couldn't handle the whole estate and Alexa knew that."

"Pretend you're going to take the case," Diane said. "What would you want to know first?"

"Let's look at it from another angle," Katie said, surprised that Diane could discuss her mother's murder in such a pragmatic manner. "Instead of thinking of what the inheritors stood to gain, let's think about what each had to lose, had the new will been legalized."

"I would have lost several million dollars," Diane said. "I'm not sure of the exact amount. Mother had lots of investments and she earmarked much of her estate for me, or for my children in the event of my death."

"Randy?" Katie asked. "What would you have lost under the terms of the new will?"

"I don't deny that I would have hated to see it go into effect. Chitting Marina now goes to Po, and I think he'll want me to help him operate it. I've been looking forward to that opportunity, which I'd have lost under the new document."

"*Think* he'll want you to help him!" Beck said. "Dear child, you *know* he will. A dilettante writer who's been pretending to create a novel for twenty years isn't likely to toss his word processor into the sea just because he's inherited a marina."

"Dad might surprise you some day," Diane said. "People see him as a lazy don't-rock-the-boat type who's always played understudy to Mother, but he just might finish that novel. It could be a best seller. Stranger things have happened."

"Dreamer," Beck said. "It's surprising how long it takes to finish a task you're not really working on."

"Anyone else who'd have lost a lot, had the new will been valid?" Katie spoke quickly, wondering how Diane tolerated Beck's comments. She knew they walked together each morning, but surely Beck must be living a foot-into-mouth existence where Diane was concerned.

"Tyler Parish," Randy said. "Put him high on your list."

"I mentioned him to you," Diane said, "Mother's . . . lover. Few artists can make a living on their own. Under the new will, Tyler would have lost Mother's gifts, as well as her social and moral support."

"Or immoral support," Beck said. "Depends on how you view it. Alexa and Tyler flouted the rules and openly flaunted their relationship."

"Did Tyler have other women friends?" Katie asked.

"Does a shark have teeth?" Beck snorted. "Had Alexa known, she would have wreaked ruin on her rivals."

"But she didn't know," Randy said. "Her ego blocked her vision."

"That's something I could investigate," Beck said. "I could ferret out names. Places. Dates."

Diane scowled. "I suppose there could be a woman out there who might have killed in order to prevent Tyler's inheritance from going to the Preservation Group."

"And then there's Alexa's secretary." Randy opened the refrigerator, pulled out another beer, popped the top. "She had a lot to lose. Personally, I think Mary Bethel's an arrogant goldbrick, but she deserves a medal for working for Alexa. What a rotten job. The woman was a bitch."

Katie glanced at Diane to see how she was taking Randy's tirade.

"We all know Mother had her faults," Diane said. "I'll be first to admit that she was demanding and hard to please."

"Why do you call Mary Bethel a goldbrick?" Katie asked.

"When I worked at the marina, she was always calling in sick or coming in late. Strange part of it was that Alexa put up with her malingering. Not like Alexa to give an inch in any direction."

"Now Randy," Diane sighed.

Randy gulped half of his beer. "I owe Alexa a lot, at that. If I could have stood working with her at the marina, I'd still be there. I'd never have struck out on my own as a backwater guide, and I'd never have known for sure that I could make it solo. I'd have been a parasite, depending on the Chittings' golden parachute."

Katie felt a growing respect for Randy. She could understand his need to prove himself. But then what? Surely the Chitting fortune must have seemed very attractive.

"What would Mary Bethel have lost under the new will?"

"An annual stipend," Randy said. "The woman's set for life."

"Fifty thousand a year," Diane said.

"Frugal Mary can retire and live on bonbons for the rest of her days," Randy said. "Poor little Mary. It could ruin her. Quash her incentive."

"Sour grapes." Diane patted Randy's hand. "I don't begrudge Mary her stipend. She always played servant to Mother, she thought so much of her. And sometimes I think Mother looked on Mary more as a daughter than as a secretary. Mary deserves her reward."

"Who's in charge of the marina at this time?" Katie asked.

"Dad's supposed to be," Diane said, "but Mary's agreed to stay until the end of the month. Between the two of them and the dockmasters, business will continue."

"There's another person involved in all this that you've forgotten to consider," Beck said.

"Who's that?" Randy asked. "Nobody else was mentioned in Alexa's will."

"Right, but another person profited from it."

Everyone waited, looking at Beck.

"Who?" Katie asked.

"Rex Layton. Think about it. The mayor stands strongly behind the Cayo Hueso Housing Project. If Alexa's estate had gone to the Preservation Group, it's almost certain that they could have hired lawyers to help them block the Cayo Hueso development."

"You'll have to fill me in," Katie said. "I haven't kept up with city politics enough to know the extent of Mayor Layton's interest in Cayo Hueso."

"Dear child, it's fairly simple. As mayor, Rex wants to see Key West grow. One way to promote growth is to provide economical housing for people. You can hardly buy a home in a decent area of the city for under two hundred thou. And rentals cost megabucks because the tourists dance to the landlord's tune. There's scant housing available to the low-income wage earner."

"And the Preservation Group disliked a housing project that would help the common laborer?" Katie suddenly felt catapulted to Rex's side concerning the Cayo Hueso project. Laborers had wives and kids, and those families deserved decent and affordable living accommodations.

She remembered the inner city in a tough part of Miami. Kids deserved better. She was about to speak out in Rex's behalf, then reconsidered. It would be unprofessional to drag personal feelings into a murder investigation.

"Do you really think Rex Layton should be considered a suspect?" Katie asked Beck.

"I wouldn't have mentioned his name if I didn't think there was a chance of his guilt."

The more Katie heard about the murder, the more it intrigued her. Could she handle this? If she could prove herself capable of solving this murder, maybe she would feel competent as a detective. Maybe she could rationalize running away from teaching.

Beck stood and headed for the door. "Think about this case, Detective Katie Hassworth. Can you really turn your back on it? Can you really go about your life with Alexa Chitting's murderer at large?"

Chapter Five

Katie helped Diane rinse the teacups and place them in the dishwasher while Beck drove Randy to get Katie's car and luggage. They talked a bit longer, then once Katie had her suitcase, she climbed the baronial staircase to the second floor. She paused for a moment to adjust the gold frame on an ancestral portrait and smooth the fringe on a French tapestry before she went on up the wide carpeted steps to her third-floor apartment.

Diane admitted feeling guilty about spending so much on antiques, admitted using Katie's rent payments to support her habit. Katie didn't mind. She admired Diane for choosing a home and family career and living on Randy's income. She wondered if everyone felt guilty about something. She also wondered how she could have been so lucky as to have met Diane. They needed each other.

The wind howled under the eaves of the third floor that consisted of one large room where, at the turn of the century, the original owners once held fancy dress balls. Tonight it smelled musty from having been closed, and

49

she opened a window a crack.

A small closet at the end of the room held ladder-like steps leading to a widow's walk on the roof. There, old-time ship captains had paced, scanning the sea for sailboats wrecked on the reef, knowing that the first captain to offer aid owned salvage rights to the distressed vessel. Sometimes Katie climbed up for a panoramic view of the island. But not tonight. Too cold. Too windy.

In her apartment, Kirman carpet designated the living area with its furniture from Diane's favorite Napoleon II era. The old rug felt soft under Katie's feet as she kicked off her shoes and turned on a lamp. Sometimes she felt almost smothered in antiques.

French screens separated the living area from the sleeping area with its burnished brass bed and the ancient dresser that had a top drawer that pulled out to form a desk. Katie unpacked, hanging her clothes in the mirrored armoire before she took a shower and climbed into bed. Then she got up again and stepped onto the bedside scales.

"One hundred twenty-five." Up a pound. Drat. The morning and night weighing-in had become a ritual. Compulsive behavior, her Miami therapist had said. She had long ago given up trying to break the habit, but she tried not to let the numbers on the scales control her life. Tomorrow she would eat nutritious meals. Fruit. Skim milk. Good low-cal stuff like that. Tomorrow. The promise palliated her conscience and she climbed into bed again. It had been a long day.

Sleep eluded her as she wondered if she could handle a murder investigation. Most of their cases so far had involved searching for missing people or tracking down information in Miami or Tallahassee concerning embezzlements. She hoped the police were right, that some drug-crazed addict had murdered Alexa. What would she do if the culprit turned out to be a respected family member? Would she be putting her own life in danger if her investigation threatened to disclose the murderer?

On Sunday Katie slept late, untroubled by the recurring nightmare which sometimes plagued her, the dream in which she relived the classroom-shooting scene. The thought of it made her shudder, but she came to life as her telephone rang. Before answering, she propped herself on one elbow and raised the window shade. The wind no longer howled, but the skies looked like molten lead.

"Hope I didn't wake you." Diane's voice greeted her. "But I know you haven't had time to grocery shop, and we have a breakfast overload. I'm bringing you a tray."

"You're a doll. I'm starving and the cupboard's bare."

"Of course my generosity's also a bribe."

"Unfair."

"I'm kidding. But I hope you like French toast with my own special guava syrup, bacon, scrambled eggs, cereal, milk, and orange juice."

"Really playing the Happy Homemaker to the hilt, aren't you?" Katie laughed, but her mouth watered.

"Did you think anymore about taking the case?"

"Yes. I had insomnia from thinking about it. But I still need to talk to Mac before we make a decision."

"We need you, Katie."

"Maybe less than you think."

Diane brought the breakfast tray, then hurried off to join Randy and the kids for church. After eating with a gusto that threatened to add pounds, Katie stood before the mirrored armoire, studying her figure. No, she wasn't fat. She remembered days at the orphanage when food had always been in short supply. The minute she had a job and left there, she indulged herself in fruit, meat, desserts. In a matter of only a few weeks, her weight had soared.

This morning, once she finished eating, she drove to the Winn Dixie and laid in a supply of groceries. It took two trips up the stairs to get them all into her tiny kitchen. Then, as she drove to her office, Bubba appeared from a side street, looking like the inventor of sleaze.

"Hey, Blondie. How about a lift to the beach?"

He had to have been waiting for her, like a frog waiting for a fly. Why walk when good old Katie Hassworth provided free transportation? She pulled to the curb and stopped long enough for him to get in. His greasy hair hung around his shoulders, and the sun peeking through the clouds glinted on his ear stud. Today he wore his shirt tucked into his jeans and secured with a black rope. All that sartorial splendor to celebrate Sunday?

She smiled at the thought as he sniffled.

"I'd like to talk with you," Katie said with feigned enthusiasm.

"I'm heading for the beach."

"It'll only take a minute or two."

"Money talk?"

"Perhaps." She drove a bit faster, reluctant to be seen with Bubba any longer than necessary. "Let's go to my office."

"Let's go to the beach. Talk goes better in sunshine and fresh air."

Katie agreed, but she drove to her office. "Business talk demands a business-like atmosphere." She parked in the scant driveway, opened the office door, and tried not to wrinkle her nose at the stale cigarette odor. Sitting at her oak desk, she offered Bubba the straight chair.

"Why didn't you tell me that Alexa Chitting was the 'old biddy' who was bumped off last Monday?"

"I didn't hear you offering any bread for the info. What gives? I see you got the scoop without my help."

"She was probably the wealthiest woman in Key West, and I happen to rent an apartment from her daughter. Diane wants me to investigate her mother's death."

"And that's where I come in?" Bubba grinned and jammed his hands more deeply into the pockets of his grimy jeans.

"Perhaps."

"I hate that word and you use it a lot, Blondie. I've noticed that about you."

" 'Perhaps' is better than 'no,' isn't it?"

"Not much."

"Want to forget the whole thing?" She used her schoolteacher voice. "I can do my own footwork, if necessary."

Bubba sighed. "You're a hard woman, Blondie. What do you want to know?"

"I haven't taken the case for sure."

Bubba stood. "So I'm going to the beach. Once all the clouds scatter, it's going to be a great day out there. You desk types ought to notice that now and then."

"Wait. The beach will still be there ten minutes from now."

Bubba slumped back into the chair as if his spine were made from cooked spaghetti. He sniffled again. "So what do you want to know?"

"Have you heard any talk about the murder?"

"Sure. Everyone's talking about it. Or at least they were. It's sort of old stuff by now."

"What were people saying?"

"Depends on what people you mean. Police call it a drug-related robbery. They see enough of them. They oughta know."

"And what are others saying?"

"That Mrs. Chitting was a grade-A bitch. That lots of good people out there hated her guts. That even her husband couldn't stand her. Some suggest he might have offed her. Others guess it might have been her son-in-law. Or even her daughter. Mrs. Chitting must have been a real sweetie face."

"You paint a lovely picture."

"She a friend of yours?"

"I didn't know her."

"But this daughter, this Diane, she's going to pay you to investigate, right?"

"Maybe — if I take the case."

"Money talks." Bubba smirked. "It can do strange things to people."

"No doubt you speak from experience."

Bubba shrugged. "What else do you want to know?"

"Just the street talk about Alexa Chitting's murder. What Tyler Parish does in his spare time. Any info about the Cayo Hueso housing project."

"Who's Tyler Parish?"

"A local artist. He rents space at a Simonton Street Loft."

"How much info you want?" Bubba wrinkled his forehead as if he were about to undertake a difficult and time-consuming undercover job.

"About twenty dollars worth."

"Let's see the twenty."

"When you produce, you'll see it. I'm no pay-in-advance type."

"Nice talking with you, Blondie."

Bubba rose and left. Katie smiled at his departing back. He liked to leave the impression that he had been unfairly treated and was out of her life for good, but she knew he'd be back. His kind always returned to the source of easy money. And he might have some valuable information. He was street smart. He listened, and he managed to stay out of jail. At least he had those things going for him.

After opening the mail that had stacked up, and finding mostly bills, Katie dialed Mac's Tallahassee motel, letting the phone ring twelve times before giving up. She should have known he wouldn't be hanging around his room on a Sunday.

She decided to take Bubba's advice and enjoy the outdoors and the day, but she didn't head for Smathers Beach where she might have to concentrate on avoiding Bubba. Instead she drove back home, donned her swimsuit, and spread a beach towel beside the Dades' private pool.

She hadn't intended to fall asleep, and she didn't know how long she had been dozing, but she came fully awake with a start. She saw no movement and heard no sound, yet she sensed that someone had been watching her.

Chapter Six

Katie jumped up, looking toward the street, but she saw nobody. Shivering as she clutched her beach towel around her, she hurried to the sidewalk and peered in both directions. Bubba. She thought the jeans-clad figure turning the corner was Bubba, but the androgyny of jeans and long hair made it quite possible that the person could be a girl. Why would Bubba have been watching her? Maybe he needed another ride somewhere. She scowled. Bubba gave her a pain. She tried to shrug off the incident, but after a few minutes of watching and waiting, she felt uneasy and went inside.

Late Sunday afternoon she got in touch with Mac and as soon as they had exchanged a few pleasantries, she began to prod him for information. "Why didn't you tell me Alexa Chitting had been murdered?"

"I supposed you knew about it. It made the *Herald.* Did you stop reading the papers?"

"My mind was on that forensic workshop and the reading it involved. I didn't bother to pick up a paper."

"Diane didn't call you?"

"No. I wish she had, but . . ."

"Sorry, Katie. If I'd known . . ."

"Diane said you refused to take the case. Why? Have we suddenly outgrown our need for money?"

"I was deep into the Gillian case and the Tallahassee files. There are some big bucks involved with the Gillians too, and I couldn't be in two places at the same time. You were away and not due back for a few days and . . ."

. . . and I didn't think you could handle a murder investigation on your own. Mentally she finished his statement for him, irritated at his attitude, yet knowing he might be right.

"I see." She tried not to sound miffed.

"I felt the police were handling the case adequately. That's another reason I didn't jump at the chance to take it on."

"Diane wants me to investigate for the family."

"Do it — if you think it merits an investigation. Did you know Diane's parents?"

"No. Alexa resented Diane's renting the apartment to me and refused to meet me. I guess Po rubber-stamped Alexa's decision. I've never met either of them."

"So here's your chance to meet Po, if you're interested."

"There are some singular circumstances involved in the murder."

"Take the case, Katie girl. We can always use the money. Some bucks blown on an investigation will mean little to the Chittings one way or the other."

"I wouldn't agree to investigate just for the bucks. Diane's my friend. She's sharing her home with me."

"You're still paying rent, aren't you?"

"Of course, but Diane and I care about each other and that makes a difference."

"Take the case. You won't be satisfied unless you do. Grab it. Give it your best."

"All right. I'm going to, but . . ."

"But what?"

"But taking it is more than an obligation growing from friendship. I respect your opinion, yet the fact of the two wills intrigues me, and the choice of murder weapon pricks my curiosity."

"So you're taking the case. Figure it all out."

"Who would try to settle a vendetta with a conch shell?"

"Good question. Who would? It's your challenge, Katie girl. See you in a week or so. You'll have the murderer all wrapped and tied with a pink ribbon by then."

As Katie hung up, she felt Mac's lack of enthusiasm, his doubt of her ability, and she also felt like an unprepared understudy suddenly thrust into the spotlight of center stage. But maybe this was her chance to prove herself to Mac, to Alexa's family, and, more important, to herself.

She gave Diane her decision later Sunday

night, and on Monday morning Diane set up an appointment for them to talk with Samuel Addison, her mother's lawyer. They arrived on Duval Street promptly at ten o'clock. A weathered-gray building housed the office and was set between an abandoned theater and a barbershop. A buzzer sounded as they entered a small room where potted palms and philodendrons caught the light that flooded through a plate glass window, giving the area a bright fishbowl effect.

Katie thought the man in the cream-colored suit at the desk was Mr. Addison until he spoke.

"Mrs. Dade and Miss Hassworth?"

"Yes," Diane said. "Is Mr. Addison in?"

"Yes, of course. He's expecting you." The secretary rose and opened the door leading into a somber inner office where carpet and draperies the color of dust held the stench of cigar smoke. Gray file cabinets lined one wall and floor-to-ceiling bookcases comprised the other three. There were no windows. Mr. Addison reinforced Katie's first impression of dreariness as he stepped toward them.

"Come in, my ladies."

Surprised at his courtly manner and orotund voice, Katie studied the thin hawk of a man who stepped from behind his gray steel desk. Arthritis had disfigured his finger joints until shaking hands with him was like gripping Tinker Toys. She guessed him to be in his eighties, and his gray suit and string tie seemed color coded to match his deep-set eyes and his complexion. One word flashed to her mind. Shrewd.

"I'm pleased to meet you, Mr. Addison. I'm sure Mrs. Dade has told you the nature of our business."

"Have seats, my ladies." The man retreated to a squeaky swivel chair behind his desk and smiled at Diane. "Yes, Diane has told me you're investigating her mother's death. I've been the family lawyer for years and I'll do whatever I can to help you." He turned slightly and the chair gave a protesting groan. "Alexa and I are . . . were both Conchs. We understood each other."

"I'll appreciate your help," Katie said.

"I've told Katie of the two wills," Diane said. "Now she needs to know more details."

"Right." Mr. Addison cleared his throat and looked at Katie. "I'll begin with Alexa's first will. The bulk of her estate is to be divided between Diane and Po Chitting. Po has inherited the marina and approximately ten million dollars in other assets."

"And Diane?"

"Diane inherits stocks and bonds valued at about fifteen million dollars. Of course, there are taxes to be figured. It will take me some time to reach a to-the-penny amount."

"That won't be necessary for my purposes." Katie tried to keep a calm expression although she found such amounts of money almost beyond her comprehension. "And Tyler Parish? Diane says he inherits a lump sum of two hundred and fifty thousand dollars."

"That's correct," Mr. Addison said.

"He could live off the interest from a sum like that," Diane said.

"Perhaps." Mr. Addison gave a thin chuckle. "The interest would never, however, allow him to live in the style he now enjoys."

"But the potential loss of such a sum might motivate a person to murder," Katie said.

"I prefer to avoid such speculation, but I do know that Parish's paintings have been catching on with the public. He's presented several shows around the country — Chicago, New York. His work is selling, though for many, his artistic expression remains numinous."

Feeling rebuked, Katie changed the subject. "Mary Bethel. I understand she'll receive an annual stipend of fifty thousand dollars. Is that correct?"

"It is," Mr. Addison said.

This time, although Katie kept her speculations to herself, she felt this shrewd old man could see into her thoughts and she found that disconcerting. "Mr. Addison, I understand that Mary Bethel was a devoted and competent secretary, but to receive such a stipend from an employer is most unusual. Do you know Miss Bethel's age?"

"I believe she's around thirty-one."

"A young person," Katie said. "If her life span matches that of the insurance charts, she will collect hundreds of thousands of dollars."

"That is correct."

"Do you know why Alexa Chitting was so generous to Mary Bethel?"

He paused, glancing uneasily at Diane. "Yes. I'm privy to that information."

"And will you reveal it?"

"Until now, it's been a matter between me and Alexa. Since Diane has asked me to help you, I'll detail the facts of Mary Bethel's inheritance if Diane gives me permission."

"Of course," Diane said, leaning forward in her chair.

"I want the information to go no farther than the walls of this room."

"I'll see that it doesn't." Katie sensed Diane's sudden interest.

"Alexa caused an accident about thirty years ago," Mr. Addison said. "You are too young to remember it, Diane. In fact, I doubt if Alexa ever told you about it."

"So tell me now," Diane said. "Surely I've a right to any and all information that concerns Mother's will — and perhaps her death."

"I'll tell you the facts as I know them, my ladies. Alexa was at the wheel of a speedboat returning from a pleasure outing at Dry Tortugas. It was after dark and both she and Po had been drinking. Her speedboat crashed into the small fishing ketch Mary Bethel's parents were in. Neither Alexa nor Po were seriously injured, but both of Mary's parents died, leaving Mary orphaned at the age of one year."

"How terrible." Stress roughened Diane's voice.

"Yes. Tragic," Mr. Addison agreed. "There were no relatives to bring suit, and the Chittings, with my help, hushed up the details of the accident. Ever since that night, Alexa tried to expiate her crime."

"How?" Katie asked.

"She provided money for Mary's support in a foster home. At one time Mary was very ill with a high fever. Fact is, she was hospitalized for weeks and the doctors thought she might die. Alexa paid all her medical expenses. She also educated her in private schools and sent her to college. Later, she employed her at the marina at a wage few secretaries ever hope to receive."

"It seems strange that a college educated woman would be content working as a secretary where chances of advancement were nonexistent," Diane said.

"Mary majored in journalism, but she dreamed of being a novelist. The secretarial job gave her an income while she free-lanced her work."

"I know Mother catered to Mary concerning office hours," Diane said. "She said that

Mary did impeccable work, but I doubt that she ever put in a forty-hour week."

"So far she has seen little success as a novelist, although she does sell an article to magazines now and then."

Katie regretted causing Diane more grief and she tried to change the subject. "Is there anyone else who might have been affected by Alexa's second will?"

Mr. Addison lit a cigar, then looked at the ceiling for several moments before he replied. "I suppose Po's lady friend would have hated to see all that money go to the Preservation Group."

"Po's lady friend?" Katie asked. "Who . . ."

"Her name?" Diane leaned forward again. "I didn't know that Dad . . . her name?"

"I'm sorry, Diane, but I don't know the woman's name."

Again Katie regretted touching on subject matter that fragmented Diane's composure. "Mr. Addison, will you outline the terms of Alexa's second will, the unsigned document?"

"It was a simple will. In essence she left one dollar each to her husband, her daughter, her grandchildren, Tyler Parish, and Mary Bethel. She left the bulk of her estate to the Key West Preservation Group."

"One dollar to family and friends?" Katie asked. "Was that intended as an insult?"

"She certainly was unhappy with her family when she decided to change her will, but she acted more in anger at the circumstances concerning her health than as an insult to anyone. Had she left these people nothing, one or all of them might have tried to break the will, claiming she was mentally incompetent and had forgotten them." Mr. Addison shoved his chair back. "Unless you have more questions, I feel there's nothing additional I can tell you, my ladies."

"Thank you for your time," Diane said. "Please send me your bill."

"This one's on the house, Diane. I'm happy to assist you. It would pleasure me to see Alexa's murderer meet justice."

"I appreciate your help, Mr. Addison," Katie said, "but one more thing. Would you request a copy of the police report of the murder? You could get it more easily than I."

"Yes. I'll request it and I'll mail it to your office. Please feel free to call on me again if you have further questions."

"Thank you." Katie stood and she and Diane left the office.

Chapter Seven

As they stepped back outside, Katie avoided Diane's eyes, but once they were inside the car, Katie took her hand and met her gaze. "I'm so very sorry you had to hear all that. Had I known what was coming, I'd have arranged to talk with Addison privately."

"I needed all that info," Diane said. "It explains many things about Mother's relationship with Mary that I've wondered about. And as for Dad . . ." Her voice trailed away. "I'm surprised that he had or has a paramour, yet why should I be? I doubt that he and Mother had slept together for years. Only a true ascetic would put up with that sort of situation."

"I'll have to learn her name," Katie said.

"Of course. But right now, why don't I drive you to see Mother's office? Would that be the next step to take?"

"Is this a convenient time for you?"

"Yes. You'll need to see the scene of the crime sooner or later, so why procrastinate?"

"Then let's go."

Diane drove the short distance through Old Town and on to the marina along horse and buggy streets so narrow they made it a challenge to avoid fender-to-fender encounters with tourists who drove their self-contained houses on wheels as if they owned the island. When they reached the marina, Diane parked in the slot marked ALEXA CHITTING. Beneath the bold letters and in smaller print were the words: "Don't even think of it."

"This must be hard for you, Diane. I'll make it brief."

"You needn't hurry. I'm trying to make peace with myself concerning Mother's death. Little by little I'm succeeding."

They sat in the car for a few moments viewing the scene. Screaming gulls and pelicans soared on the tradewind like animated kites above the blue and white marina structures that comprised a city within a city. On past the hotel area, Katie could see an outdoor café and bar, a ship's store, and rental kiosks which offered ten-speed bicycles, mopeds, and wind surfers. A marina spelled big business.

A breeze carried mingled smells of salt air and orange juice, diesel fuel and coffee, hemp rope and cinnamon rolls. They watched the motley group who had been attracted to the area — tourists, marina patrons and employees, and local Conchs who chose to sun themselves on Chitting benches that overlooked the boardwalk and the sea. Knowing that a murderer had struck only a few feet above this halcyon scene sobered Katie and left her feeling wary and vulnerable.

"Mother and I weren't close," Diane said as they sat there. "Everyone knows that. I suppose our estrangement was as much my fault as hers."

"You needn't talk about it. I know it's painful."

"You'll hear about it from others once you start probing. I'd rather you heard it from me. And I want you to know right off that I was at a City Council meeting during the time of the murder. So was Rex Layton. Beck might as well forget the mayor as a suspect. Rex presided at the meeting, and I have lots of people who will vouch for his presence — and mine."

"Why didn't you say so when Beck suggested Rex's name?"

"She'd probably have said he could have slipped out of the meeting and then returned. No point in starting an argument with her. Sometimes she can be an I'll-have-the-last-word-or-else type."

"Could Rex have left the meeting and then returned?"

"Hardly. As mayor, he held the gavel. He stood right there in front of everyone all evening as he presided over the meeting."

"I'll check that out later. Tell me about your mother."

"Mother always tried to dominate me." Diane sighed. "From the time I was a teenager, I rebelled. We went through the eastern boarding school scene, the Ivy League college scene. After I graduated from Wellesley, she insisted that I be her business partner at the marina because I had earned my M.B.A."

"That surprises me." She couldn't imagine Diane as a businesswoman — unless she ran an antique store or an interior decorating shop. "The M.B.A., I mean, not the fact that Alexa wanted you as her partner."

"It galled Mother that I never used my degree. She tried to prevent my marriage — hated Randy on sight. I suppose we should have lived somewhere else, but we both love Key West. When Mother finally accepted our marriage as a hard fact of her life, she let Randy take over the buying for the marina. It could have been an ideal situation."

"But he hated it, right?"

"Right. He *abhorred* working for her. He finally quit, and Mother ostracized him completely. I suppose you can't rule Randy out as a suspect, can you?"

Suddenly Katie felt on guard. Diane was right. She couldn't count Randy out, but she refused to think about that now. She hated having to consider friends as suspects. "I'll be talking to everyone who was close to Alexa."

"Of course. I should have been a better daughter. I could have pulled in my horns and done more to keep the family ties from fraying. Had I done so, there might never have been that second will — or the murder."

"Don't blame yourself. It's pointless. All of Alexa's associates are probably thinking of things they could have done that *might* have prevented the tragedy. Ease up."

"I'll try."

They left the car and crossed the parking lot.

"This way." Diane followed a narrow cement strip until they reached a wide-planked boardwalk built on pilings above the sea. Feeling the gentle sway underfoot, Katie reached for the weathered hemp line suspended between black iron posts that served as a barrier between land and water. Here the strong smell of diesel fuel and salt air mingled as sailboats, fishing crafts, and cabin cruisers rocked gently in the maze of slips extending far into the bight.

"Chitting Marina does a big business," Katie commented.

"Right. It's usually crowded here. Many incoming captains radio the dockmaster for slip reservations much as motorists make hotel reservations, but some local boat owners rent their slips by the month or by the year."

They watched while a dockmaster wearing white slacks and a black sweatshirt bearing the words CHITTING MARINA helped a captain ease his craft into a slip and hook up with the electric power line. Pocketing his tip, the dockmaster looked up and smiled at Diane.

"May I be of help, Mrs. Dade?"

"No thanks, Ben. We're on our way to Mother's office for a few moments." Turning, she led Katie to the elevator and they rode to the third floor. The slight, dark-haired girl at the desk looked up as they entered the office. For an instant, upon seeing Diane, she sat so still she might have been a picture freeze-framed by a video camera. Then she relaxed, smiled, and stood.

"Katie, I'd like you to meet Mary Bethel, Mother's secretary. Mary, this is Katie Hassworth. She's with the McCartel and Hassworth Detective Agency and she's investigating Mother's death."

Small boned and fragile looking, Mary Bethel, with her stark black dress and ebony hair and eyes, reminded Katie of a figure in one of the dainty turn-of-the-century silhouettes mounted under convex glass in Diane's bedroom.

After they exchanged greetings, Mary looked directly at Katie. "I suppose you want to question me."

"Perhaps. But not now. Today I'm here to observe the office."

Katie thought Mary looked relieved, but she could hardly blame her. Nobody enjoyed being interrogated about a murder.

"I'll be available whenever you want to talk with me," Mary said. "I want to see Alexa's killer caught. Alexa was a wonderful person and a perfect boss. I'd still be starving as a free-lance writer if she hadn't provided this job. I'm deeply in her debt."

Katie studied Mary. Could she and Randy Dade have worked for the same woman, the bitch Bubba had so eloquently described? If Mary was trying to cloak herself in innocence, she was overacting.

"The family appreciates your carrying on with the business," Diane said. "Katie will be in touch later. And Mary, you needn't continue wearing those black dresses."

"I enjoy the dresses, and discarding them would be a waste. I think Alexa would have wanted me to continue wearing them. They were her idea."

Katie watched for Diane's reaction to Mary's patronizing tone and manner, but there was none, and she had to admit that the tailored dress matched Mary's every-hair-in-place coiffure in a flattering way.

Mary sat down and began typing, and Katie studied the office, ticking off the accouterments in her mind. Picture window like a giant eye overlooking the boat slips. White carpet. Walls covered in a textured white silk. White satin draperies. Black leather couch and easy chairs. She was struck by the stark black and white in this Chitting world where sea blue might have seemed more appropriate.

The deep-piled carpet cushioned her steps

74

as she approached the walnut desk across the spacious room from Mary Bethel's work area. Beneath Alexa's swivel chair rusty-brown stains marred the carpet, and blood had also splattered the wall.

"Alexa and Mary always shared the office?" Katie glanced at Diane, who kept her gaze averted from the stains.

"Yes. Mother liked to have Mary close at hand." She stepped to the left of the desk and opened a narrow door. "They have a bathroom here."

Katie inspected the room, noting the usual fixtures one might find in any bathroom. "The police went over the room carefully, I suppose."

"Yes. They said they found prints from only Mother and Mary. The killer must have worn gloves."

"That figures." A black-bordered Oriental carpet dominated the wall behind Alexa's desk, and to one side of it hung a gold-framed seascape.

"There's a wall safe behind the painting."

Katie eased the frame aside. "Who had access to the safe?"

"Mother, Mary, and Dad. Do you want it opened?"

"Not today." The gilt-framed seascape with the name T. Parish slanted across the lower right corner looked as if it might have been lifted directly from Alexa's gilt-edged life, but the Oriental carpet hanging next to it seemed more appropriate for Diane's home than for this office. Both hangings seemed at odds with the black and white office décor.

Katie straightened the seascape, then studied the Oriental carpet with its wines, blues, greens and its black border which supported heavy fringe that hung like short-cropped hair. "A lovely piece."

"Yes," Diane agreed. "Antique, of course. I gave it to Mother for her last birthday. I intended it for her home, but she preferred to hang it here."

"Then you weren't totally estranged. You did converse and exchange gifts."

"Yes. But usually the gifts were more like unsuccessful peace offerings."

Katie stepped behind the desk and continued to study the carpet, touching the luxurious nap. Was it a twin to the one in her apartment? Seeing nothing unusual about the hanging rug, she was about to turn aside when she felt a slight roughness in the pile. A closer look revealed an almost imperceptible flaw in the thick nap of the black border. A bullet hole? She stepped back to the front of the desk.

"Where's the conch shell?"

"The police have it. Do you need to examine it?"

"I may ask to see it when I talk with the police."

"There were no fingerprints on it other than Mother's."

"Who has the keys to this office?"

"I'm not sure." Diane turned to Mary. "Mary, do you know who has the keys to this office?"

"Alexa had one, of course. And Po. And I have one. Each dockmaster also had a key and there was a master key in the dockmaster's office."

"How many dockmasters work here?"

"Ten," Mary replied. "Of course, they work different shifts."

"So anyone having access to the dockmaster's office would have access to the key to this office?" Katie asked.

"Yes," Mary said. "Alexa wanted it that way. Anything important she kept in the safe, but sometimes she needed a dockmaster to run an errand for her and sometimes the errand would require entering this office when neither she nor I was present."

"I see," Katie said. "Did Alexa call on the dockmasters to do errands for her frequently?"

Mary thought for a few moments. "I wouldn't say frequently, but she did call on them occasionally. Alexa enjoyed delegating duties."

Katie wondered if she heard a note of sarcasm in Mary's voice. "Mary, could you get me the dockmasters' keys to this office?"

"Right now?"

"Yes, please. I'd like to examine them."

"Of course. I'll go to the dockmaster's office myself. The guys down there will know where the keys are and they owe me some favors. Excuse me, please." She rose from her desk, closing its top drawer before she left the room.

"Diane, could you get your father's key to this office?"

"Yes, of course. Will you be looking for fingerprints?"

"Perhaps. Sometimes I don't know what I'm looking for until I see it."

Katie waited until Mary and Diane were gone, then she strode to Mary's desk and tried the top drawer. It didn't surprise her to find it locked and she wondered what Mary had in there that she preferred nobody to see.

Hurry. She had to act before they returned. Crossing the room, she lifted the lower right corner of the Oriental hanging. To her surprise she found no bullet hole in the wall. Examining the carpet more carefully, she touched the hole in the nap and then she felt a leather label on the back of the rug, realizing the leather had stopped the bullet. She left the bullet where it was in case she might need it for evidence later. When Mary and Diane returned, she pretended to be examining the lock on the bathroom door.

"Here are two keys." Mary laid the keys on

her desk. "The head dockmaster will leave the others as soon as he can round them up."

Diane added a third key to the group, and Katie went to the desk, picked up each key and examined it carefully.

"Do you see anything unusual about the keys?" Diane asked.

Katie shook her head then turned aside. "I'd rather not say right at this moment." She laid the keys back on Mary's desk. "Thank you both for your trouble. You may return the keys at your convenience, Mary. I think I've seen enough for today and I appreciate your cooperation."

She turned to Diane. "Shall we go now?"

Katie felt Mary's gaze follow them from the office and she wondered if the secretary was watching them from the picture window. When they got off the elevator and stepped onto the boardwalk, she looked up at the office again, but no one was in sight.

Chapter Eight

After Diane let Katie out at her office, Katie considered the bullet. The police had overlooked this piece of evidence; surely they would have taken the bullet with them had they been aware of it.

During the afternoon she made notes on things she had seen and heard at Samuel Addison's office and at the Chitting Marina. Mary Bethel had praised Alexa and she had been civil to Diane, but Katie wished she knew more about Mary. Did the two women resent each other? According to Samuel Addison, Alexa had done everything but invite Mary into the Chitting home as a daughter.

If the aperture in the wall hanging had been made the night of the murder, surely the killer had come armed with intent, changed his mind and substituted the conch shell for the gun. Why? Fury? Had hate of Alexa burgeoned into fury? Had the killer lost control and seized the conch shell when the bullet went astray? Surely the gun had held more than one bullet.

When no answers were forthcoming, Katie let her mind roam to other matters. Picking up the telephone directory, she looked up a number and dialed.

"Ty Parish here." His voice boomed over the line.

"Katie Hassworth speaking, Mr. Parish. I'm a private detective hired by the Chitting family and I'd like to talk with you."

"I'll just bet you would."

"When could we set up an appointment?"

"I didn't say I'd talk to you."

"But I'm hoping you will. Surely you want the person or persons who killed Mrs. Chitting brought to justice."

"Yes, indeed. I'd like that very much. Alexa Chitting meant a lot to me in many ways."

"Then let's set a time to talk. Any light you might be able to shed on the case will be a help."

"I've already talked to the police. They have a record of everything I said. Can't you contact them? I've nothing more to say than what I've told them and I'm a busy man."

"I need to talk with you personally. You set the time — at your convenience, of course."

"Of course."

She heard the sarcasm followed by silence and the hollow hum of the line. "Mr. Parish?"

"Yes, Miss Hassworth. I'm thinking about your request."

Now his voice was smoother and she tried to imagine just how he might look. Tall. Slim. Dark hair. Slender fingers. A bit frail.

She recalled the rerun of an old David Niven movie and imagined Tyler Parish as a David Niven type — handsome and sophisticated. She could imagine him and Alexa together, turning heads wherever they went.

"Mr. Parish, when would it be convenient for you to meet with me?"

"Look, I'm really snowed under. You've called at a very busy time."

"Then I'll call back later on a more convenient day."

"No. No. Don't call me. I'll call you."

"That word package has a familiar ring. Let's not play games."

"I have a one-man show on Thursday night at East Martello. Surely you've read about it. I'll be terribly busy until after that's over. I'm framing. I'm hanging. I'm still painting on two of the oils. I promise I'll call you on Friday — Saturday at the latest."

"Thank you. That will be fine and I'll look forward to meeting you." She replaced the receiver, knowing she wouldn't hear from Tyler Parish again unless she instigated another call. She was still thinking of him when the telephone rang and Rex Layton's voice flowed across the wire. She smiled and leaned forward. "How may I help you, Mayor?"

"Rex, Katie. Please call me Rex — and this is strictly an unofficial call. I understand there's an excellent new chef cooking at

Louie's Back Yard these evenings and I'd like to take you to dinner if you're free tonight."

Part of her wanted to blurt no. She had a plethora of problems to think about that needed her undivided attention. But another part of her verbalized deeper feelings. "How nice, Rex. I'd love to have dinner with you, but I'm warning you — I'm starving."

"I always take starving women to Louie's. May I pick you up at your house around seven?"

"That would be fine."

"I hear you're investigating the Chitting case."

"News travels." She straightened in her chair. "Who told you?"

"I'll reveal all over dinner, but I doubt you'll be too surprised. See you then."

"Thanks, Rex."

After replacing the receiver, she stared dreamily at the telephone for a few seconds before she turned back to her work at hand. She made out a time sheet for the day, noting to whom she had talked and the gist of the conversation. Mac would want to see it when he returned, and she would give a copy to the Chitting family once she was off the case.

Going home from the office Katie asked herself why she had accepted Rex's invitation. She had promised herself after the divorce never to get involved with another man.

Never ever. She didn't need men to make her life meaningful. But Rex fascinated her. Why would a man who could have his choice of Key West ladies notice her? It pleased her to be able to tell him she was starving. Sometimes facing her appetite helped her control it. She hadn't seen her therapist for over a year, and her last contact with Overeaters Anonymous had been six months ago. She parked her convertible under the sea grape tree in front of the house and grinned at Diane who was standing in the doorway.

"Did Rex reach you?"

"How did you know?"

"He called here, supposedly about a council meeting, then he casually mentioned that he'd tried your office and couldn't get you. I told him to try again, that you usually checked in there before you came home for the day. Are you having dinner with him?"

"You're intuitive."

Diane opened the door for her and followed her to the staircase. "You'll make a scintillating couple."

"You haven't been playing matchmaker, have you?" Katie studied Diane for a moment. "You married types are never satisfied until everyone's wearing a wedding band."

"Just want you to enjoy the finer things in life." Diane walked on toward the kitchen. "Have fun. Rex is really a nice guy."

"I'll keep that in mind."

She showered, brushed her hair until it gleamed, then put on fresh makeup. Standing in front of the armoire she debated what to wear. The cream colored shirt and cropped top? The green shift? She decided on the green, feeling a bit guilty about so obviously playing up her eyes.

When she was ready, she picked up her green sweater and went to the front veranda. She saw Rex drive up in his silver Corvette before he saw her. White silk slacks, white shirt, navy jacket. His hair fascinated her. It lay so thick that it seemed more like a pelt than hair. She watched the way he moved. Graceful. Lynx-like and very sure of himself. She stood as he approached the porch steps.

"I like a woman who's on time."

"Hunger does that to me. I warned you."

They drove across the island to the old mansion that had been turned into an elegant oceanside restaurant, and the hostess seated them on the torchlit terrace where they could watch moonlight filter through palm fronds and where waves frothed against the beach. A pianist inside the house played pop tunes from the Forties, and the music served as background for the muted voices of the other diners.

"It's almost a cliché, isn't it?" Rex asked after the hostess seated them. "I could buy a reproduction of this scene on a postcard at any shop on Front Street."

"But it's a lovely cliché, and I wouldn't have it any other way." She inhaled the scent of gardenia and touched the waxy blossom floating in a crystal bowl at the center of their table. "That flower looks too perfect to be real."

"And so do you."

"Flattery, flattery." She laughed, but she felt her face flush and she hoped he wouldn't notice. Once the waiter had gone to bring their wine, she smiled at him as she enjoyed the scene at hand. "It's hard to imagine a murder taking place on an island that offers so much beauty and loveliness."

"Even paradise has its flaws. Guess the loveliness tends to make the flaws all the more obscene."

Katie eased her sweater around her shoulders. "Who told you I was taking the Chitting case?"

"Three guesses."

"Diane?"

"No."

"Po?"

"Guess again."

"Bubba?"

"Right. So be warned. That guy works both sides of the street."

"Guess there's no law against it. But in the future I'll be even more circumspect about what I tell him."

"Do you really think you can uncover information the police have missed?"

"Perhaps. Alexa's dead and somebody killed her. Maybe the police gave up too soon."

Rex looked directly at her. "Are you suggesting that maybe it was to their advantage to go easy in their investigation?"

A warning bell sounded in her mind. "Why would you ask that?"

"Because drug money talks, that's why. We both know that. Maybe some money changed hands and closed mouths."

"I'll consider that theory. There are lots of things to think about."

"In a nice sort of way, you're telling me to mind my own business, right?"

"Of course not. I've only started working on the case, and there really *are* a lot of things to think about. I wish Mac were back."

"Any chance he'll show soon?"

"None. Enough about murder. Tell me about *your* work. How is the housing project coming along? Cayo Hueso? Isn't that what it's called?"

He leaned back in his chair and she saw the familiar gesture of strong fingers raking through thick hair. Strong hands for that matter. It would take strong hands to kill someone with a conch shell. She forced her attention back to his words about the project.

"Yes, Cayo Hueso — an archaic name for

Key West. I think the project's going to go in the near future, although I was worried for a while."

"Had Alexa's new will gone into effect, it could have made a big difference to you, couldn't it? If fortified with big money, the Preservation Group might have had the clout to save the salt pond area."

"Can't deny that. But there were other problems, too."

"Give me a for instance. I'm really not into all the intricate politics involved in city housing."

"For instance, Elizabeth Wright." Rex sipped his wine then continued. "She's head of the Florida Task Force on Key West Development and she manages the local Department of Community Affairs. Elizabeth's decisions carry lots of weight both here and in Tallahassee."

She felt herself tense at the mention of Elizabeth's name. Was Rex in love with that woman? She remembered the way Elizabeth had linked her arm through his at the buskerfest parade. "Is Elizabeth Wright for or against Cayo Hueso?"

Rex delayed answering as the waiter approached.

"The special tonight is blackened grouper served with broccoli tips in cheese sauce and your choice of wild rice, baked potato, or French fries. Will you need more time to study the menu?"

"Katie?" Rex smiled. "What would you like?"

"The grouper, please."

"Make it two," Rex said. They gave their salad and potato preferences and resumed their conversation when the waiter left.

"For a while I thought I had Elizabeth strongly on my side. We both agreed that Key West needs suitable housing for low-income wage earners. We both agreed that there's a dearth of such housing. And we both agreed that a part of the old salt pond area would be an ideal location for such a project."

"So what happened?" Had he and Elizabeth been lovers? What did she care!

"Believe it or not, I don't know what happened." Rex set his wineglass down. "She was almost ready to sign papers that would get the project going, then with no warning she called to tell me she had changed her mind. She presented all sorts of reasons why the project was unsuitable for the salt pond location or perhaps for any other location on this crowded island."

"When exactly did that call come?"

"The Friday morning before Alexa was murdered. Reporters got hold of the information and it made banner news headlines that day — above the fold in both the *Citizen* and the *Herald*."

After the waiter served their dinners, Katie ate in silence for a few moments, letting cheese melt on her tongue, savoring its saltiness. Enough talk about Elizabeth Wright. A sense of urgency nibbled at her mind as she approached the question that had been nagging at her. "Rex, anyone who would profit by the non-implementation of Alexa's second will could be a murder suspect."

"That's true, I suppose." He smiled at her. "Are you putting me on your list of those under suspicion?"

"No." She looked directly at him. "But where were you a week ago tonight?"

He laughed, and the sound relieved the sudden tension that had grown between them. "I was presiding at a city council meeting at the courthouse. I've lots of witnesses. Diane Dade, for one. And I sat beside Samuel Addison. He'll vouch that neither of us left the room before the meeting ended a little after eleven o'clock."

"Diane told me you both attended that meeting. I just wanted to hear it from you personally." She'd check with Addison to see if he'd confirm Rex's account about not having left the meeting.

"I like a detective who's thorough."

"I'm glad. I'll check with Mr. Addison, then I'll know for sure that you don't belong on my list."

"Merely your suspect list, I hope."

"Right." Katie grinned at him, flattered at his interest in her. Or his pretend interest.

She wished she knew him better.

"Tell me. How did you happen to become a detective?"

"It's a long story. Sure you're interested?"

"Of course. Tell all." He took a sip of coffee. "Stop only if I yawn."

Katie sighed, wondering how much to tell. "Before I came to Key West, I taught school in Miami — middle school English. Then one day a suicidal student brought a gun to class, fatally wounded a classmate, shot me, then killed himself."

"My God!" Rex laid his fork down and reached for her hand. "I'm sorry. I didn't mean to pry into old traumas."

"The boy was Mac McCartel's son. Jon had been doing drugs, and Mac and I worked until we tracked down his supplier. I felt great satisfaction in that and I couldn't bear the thought of returning to the class-room, so I accepted Mac's offer to work with him here."

"I'm impressed." He picked up his fork again. "You have a lot of personal courage."

She laughed. "Perhaps not as much as you think. Does a person who's running away really have courage?"

"It depends on circumstances, I suppose."

"In the past, when anyone asked what I taught, I always said, 'kids.' Kids came first and English came second. Want to know why?"

"You haven't seen me yawn, have you?"

"Because of Miss Ludwig. She was my high school English teacher. Miss Ludwig helped me get scholarships and campus jobs, and she wouldn't let me quit college until I got my master's degree in English. When I left the classroom, I felt I had let *her* down as well as myself."

"You really enjoyed teaching?"

"Yes. I felt it was important to teach kids the fundamentals of grammar. A kid who grows up saying, 'I seen' and 'he come' and 'I have did' is saddled with a stigma that will hold him back for the rest of his life."

"Right."

"A student may hear that kind of talk at home, but a good teacher can show that student a better direction — a direction that can upgrade his life both socially and economically."

"You're right, of course."

"I believed that. I still believe it. Yet I walked out of teaching. I don't call that personal courage even though my job as a detective may be a dangerous one at times."

A tense silence grew between them until he spoke again. "There are all kinds of courage."

She regretted having sounded off. What would he think of her! She wished she didn't care. But she did.

"I didn't mean to pry so deeply into your life, but I'm glad you've told me these things. Do you enjoy being a detective?"

"Yes. I do."

"Then that's reason enough for continuing."

They finished their dinner then strolled along the water's edge for a few minutes, watching the moonlight glint against the frothing waves. Rex took her hand in his strong grip, and she didn't pull away until she had to stop and shake sand from her shoes. He held her elbow to help her keep her balance, then led her to a low seawall where they sat and watched the Atlantic.

"Do you ever wonder where those waves have been?" he asked. "Think about it. They could have washed a shore in Africa or China or . . ."

"You've a big imagination."

"I'm just a dreamer at heart."

"I suppose you believe in mermaids, too."

"The subject could be up for discussion. Nobody's proved mermaids don't exist. Just saying the word brings a picture to mind."

"That's true." She eased from the seawall. "It's getting late, Rex, and I'm a working woman."

He held her hand again as they walked to his car and when they reached the Dade home, he strolled with her to the veranda. When he took her in his arms, she relaxed in his embrace, letting her body mold to his, enjoying the touch of his hand against her hair. The warmth of his lips against hers sent a thrill through her until she reluctantly pulled away.

"Thanks for a great evening."

"I had a lovely time." She squeezed his hand. "Goodnight."

Stepping inside quickly, she hurried upstairs, wondering if their date had really been all that lovely? It had been a rubber band of an evening with tensions stretching between them, straining, relaxing, then straining again as they dodged around subjects that might snap the fragile elastic.

What must he think of her? She had spent lots of time talking about her personal life without giving him much chance to tell her about his. Could a man forgive that? Had he known of her failed marriage, would it have put him off? She still felt the brush of his lips and she hoped he would call her again.

Chapter Nine

Katie lay staring at the ceiling a long time that night, thinking about Rex Layton, denying her attraction to him, then admitting that attraction but promising herself she would accept no more dates with him. She wouldn't get involved. She wasn't ready. It would be unfair for her to continue to see him. Then she laughed at herself. What made her think Rex would call her again, since he divided his time among a bevy of women? She heard the grandfather clock on the second floor strike two before she fell asleep.

Palm fronds and mahogany branches lashing against her windows wakened Katie on Tuesday morning as another front howled through the Keys. Turning on her radio, she heard the weatherman stoically warn that there might be no warm-up before the weekend. Winter! But maybe the forecast was wrong. At times the weather ignored the predictor.

She made herself a light breakfast then drove to the Monroe County library in the heart of Old Town. Here giant cacti flanked many of the frame Conch houses that lined the narrow streets, their steep tin roofs, second-story verandas, and gingerbread trim giving the tourists fresh subject matter for their cameras. She parked in front of the pale stucco building that looked as if it might have dropped from storybook land and hurried up a short flight of steps, stopping at the main desk just inside the front door. The room felt hot and stultifying, and the ever-present smell of books and bindings and inked pages blended with the sound of hushed voices. Library. She loved its protected velvet-bubble ambience.

"Do you have past issues of the *Key West Citizen*?" she asked a page.

"Yes, Ma'am." The woman rose lethargically from her chair. "What dates, please?"

How long had the Cayo Hueso dispute been going on? "The last month, please. I'll start there."

"Follow me. I'll get the papers for you."

She followed the page to a reading table, sat down, and waited. Presently, the woman returned, stacking a pile of newspapers on the table beside her.

"Here you are, ma'am. Let me know if you need more. We have many older issues on tape."

Katie thanked the woman and began perusing front-page headlines, beginning with the Tuesday following Alexa's murder. WEALTHY BUSINESSWOMAN SLAIN. Smaller print gave the who, when, and where details, along with police speculation that the robbery had been the motive for the murder. The article then highlighted Alexa's contributions to the community and the financial success of Chitting Marina under her astute management.

She read that the medical examiner placed the time of Alexa's death early in the evening — between eight and ten o'clock. Strange, Katie thought. Surely there must have been some activity around the marina at that time. True dark fell before seven o'clock, and most boats would have been in their slips by then, but sometimes people remained aboard their crafts, entertaining guests or merely engaging in their daily routines. Surely someone must have seen or heard something unusual that night.

Rubbing her eyes, she continued reading, focusing on columns that contained the ongoing story of the Cayo Hueso Housing development. Each article recapped previous information, and gradually she got the total picture, which matched the facts Rex had told her the evening before. She stacked the papers neatly and sat thinking until the page approached.

"Do you need anything else, Ma'am?"

"Have you any information on the salt ponds?"

"I'm sure there's material on that subject in the Florida Room. Miss Glockner will help you back there."

Katie glanced at her watch. "I haven't time to look up material right now. Could you give me general information? I've lived here about two years, but I've been unaware of any salt ponds."

"I'm no historian, but I do know that in early island days the settlers trapped sea water in man-made ponds and through a process of evaporation made salt. At the time it was a needed and profitable business, but as the island developed, other enterprises proved more lucrative, and workers eventually abandoned the salt ponds."

"And now they're considered of historic interest?"

"Right. The Preservation Group's trying to protect what's left of them, and the area does provide a wildlife sanctuary, although my grandfather says he sees more birds and alligators on the golf course than he's ever seen at the salt ponds."

"Opinions differ." Katie thanked the woman and left the library, driving through the chilly morning to her office. On Simonton Street a dank wind whipped red and lavender bougainvillea blossoms against picket fences and bent scarlet hibiscus and golden alamanda bushes to the ground. She shivered as she coaxed her convertible through the congested traffic. When cold fronts kept visitors off the beaches, they took to their vans, driving endlessly around the small island. Too bad the founding fathers hadn't foreseen the tourist season and provided wider streets.

Once in her office, Katie opened the windows as she did every morning in a vain attempt to vanquish the stale smoke odor. Some days she floated a gardenia blossom on her desk to freshen the room, but she hadn't taken time to do that this morning.

"Hi, Blondie." Bubba stepped into her office, sniffling as he lowered himself onto the straight-backed chair without invitation. With his grubby jeans he wore a red gingham shirt minus buttons and knotted at the waist. Katie wondered if he had ever shaved. Or had a haircut. As a little boy, had his mother hauled him to the barber on a bi-weekly basis? The thought boggled her imagination.

"Good morning, Bubba. You're out and about early."

"Got info for you."

"I hear you also had info for Mayor Layton."

"Got to keep on the good side of the law."

Noting his obsequious tone, she automatically used her schoolteacher voice. "Mayor Layton's hardly the law."

"His money's good with me. What do you care that I told him you were on the Chitting case? He would have found out sooner or later. Don't really know why he thought it important enough to shell out cash."

She wondered the same thing. Maybe, like herself, Rex sometimes paid for chaff in hope of getting grain in the next harvest.

"I was just lucky enough to get to the good mayor first."

"I'll guard my words more carefully in the future." She continued moving papers about on her desk, wondering what information Bubba had, yet hiding her eagerness to hear it.

"Needn't get on your high horse, Blondie. Now if I worked exclusively for you, it would be different. There'd be no leaks. You'd have first shot at anything I learned. Of course, the price would go up."

"Maybe I can no longer afford you."

"Oh, come on! A wealthy detective like you? Give me a break. You want to hear what I know or not?"

"I want to hear." She hated being in the position of pandering to his laziness and greed. "What's it going to cost me?"

"A twenty. We already decided on that."

"How do I know your info's worth that?"

"We all have to take chances in this life. This is one of yours."

"Your scoop better be worth the bucks. If not, you may have trouble peddling your next load."

"It's worth it. Would I lie to you?"

"Would you?" She looked him in the eye as she pulled a twenty-dollar bill from her billfold and slapped it on the table, keeping her forefinger on Andrew Jackson's nose. "Give."

Bubba relaxed, as if to begin a long story, but he kept his gaze on the money. "Been thinking back to the night someone offed Alexa Chitting. Been searching through my mind."

She thought the area might be virtually uncongested, but she waited for him to continue.

"That night I took a stroll. I do that sometimes, you know. Stroll and think. Stroll and think. Well, that night I was strolling along Houseboat Row and I passed Po Chitting. It was before ten o'clock."

"And that's it?"

"That's it."

He reached for the twenty, but she held it to the desk. "That bit of trivia is supposed to be worth a twenty?"

"I think so. You might find it worth even more than that if you ask yourself why Po Chitting would be interested in those crummy boats along Houseboat Row. Do you think that's where he told the police he was the night of the murder? I'm guessing he told them he was home alone. Isn't that what suspects say when they have no alibi?"

"You've been reading too many detective novels." Katie relinquished the twenty and Bubba pocketed it. "Have you given the police this information?"

"Hell no." Bubba sniffled. "Don't need any truck with police . . ." He nodded toward a man approaching the office. "Here he comes now."

Bubba stood and slipped into the hallway as Po Chitting entered Katie's office.

Chapter Ten

Porter Chitting slouched his lanky frame through the doorway, ducking his head to keep from hitting it on the doorjamb as he entered Katie's office. He looked at the chair Bubba had just vacated as if he would like to wipe it off before sitting on it in his white designer slacks, but he didn't. Instead, he dropped his cold pipe into the pocket of his navy blazer and smiled. Katie counted the blazer buttons. All present. Crazy thought. Po probably owned dozens of blazers.

"Name's Po Chitting." He extended his tanned hand and Katie shook it, smelling the telltale fragrance of lime after-shave. In spite of his natty clothing, Po projected a comfortable old-shoe quality that put Katie at ease, but his slouching manner belied his strong grip. She felt her ring dig into her finger. His smile, his clear eyes, his clean-shaven face, all gave him the look of a man who was taking his bereavement in stride.

"I'm pleased to meet you, Mr. Chitting. Do sit down. Of course, I feel as if I already know you because Diane speaks of you often. I'm her third-floor renter."

Po chuckled. "I know all about Diane's

rental apartment. Drove her mother crazy. Alexa grew livid just thinking about it. Not the Chitting style to let out rooms to strangers."

When he smiled, Po's violet-colored eyes crinkled at the corners, accenting his silver hair. Katie squelched a smile. Romance heroines were supposed to have violet-colored eyes, not wealthy pseudo-novelists who displayed more knowledge about fashionable clothes and yachts than about word processors and editorial deadlines.

"I'm no longer a stranger. During the time I've lived with the Dades, Diane and I have become friends."

"So you and Diane are friends." Po shrugged. "Fine. I like your style, Katie Hassworth. I'm pleased that you're investigating Alexa's murder and I've come to give you a retainer unless Diane's already done so."

"No. We haven't discussed money."

"Very unbusinesslike of you. What's your fee for all this nosey-poking?"

"Nosey-poking?" Katie laughed at the old-fashioned term she hadn't heard or used in ages.

"Will five grand keep you on the job for a while?"

"That's very generous, Mr. Chitting."

"Po. My friends all call me Po. And we *are* going to be friends, aren't we?"

"I hope so, Mr. . . . Po." Katie found it hard to look Po in the eye because his gaze strayed around the room. "Five thousand will buy you about ten days, since my per diem fee is five hundred plus expenses."

"Bubba one of your expenses?"

"Sometimes." She waited for his objection, but none came.

"A person gleans information from whatever sources are available, I suppose. The police might have been more effective if they'd recruited Bubba for their team."

"You think they did a slipshod job?"

"Right. Otherwise, the killer would be in the slammer instead of at large."

"Many times making an arrest is a difficult thing. The police obviously felt they needed more evidence."

"I suppose you'll be wanting to question me sometime soon."

"Yes. I intend to interrogate all of Alexa's family and close associates. I know that'll involve a lot of people." She looked at Po's slender, well-manicured hands. Could they have wielded that conch shell?

"The spouse usually rates the prime spot on the suspect list from what I hear," Po said.

"Sometimes, but not always. The person who finds the body also draws major interest."

"Little Mary Bethel? I have a hard time picturing her as a killer. She's been almost like one of the family for years. You suspect Mary?"

"I didn't say that. I said that the person who finds the body is of major interest. Mary stood to profit from the existing will, didn't she? Maybe she found working as a secretary tedious."

"What makes you think she hated her job? Little Mary always seemed content working for Alexa. They were devoted to each other."

Little Mary? Why the diminutive? Did he think of her as a daughter? He didn't call Diane *Little Diane*. "I didn't say I thought Mary hated her job. I said maybe she found it tedious. Maybe. Detectives use that word a lot."

"Smart of them."

"As Alexa's secretary, Mary had access to both wills, since they were filed in Alexa's office as well as in the attorney's office. She knew that on Alexa's death she would inherit generous annual payments. Maybe she disliked the thought of losing that money."

"Nobody likes losing money."

"Maybe she wanted more time to devote to her writing."

Po flushed and looked at his left toe. "The fact that the old will is in effect certainly adds two more names to the suspect list — Rex Layton and Elizabeth Wright. Either of those two would have hated to see the Chitting money go to the Preservation Group."

"I can understand why you consider Mayor Layton a suspect. As long as most of the Chitting money stayed in the family, it wouldn't be used to fight the Cayo Hueso development he supported."

"Correct." Po stared at his right toe.

"But Elizabeth Wright? I don't understand. She had changed her mind about supporting Cayo Hueso, and at the time of Alexa's death, she seemed to be on the side of the Preservation Group."

"Not so."

"But she cited reasons why the project would be unsuitable for the salt pond area. Seems to me she would have favored the new will and that she wanted to be an ally of the Preservation Group."

"She played games," Po said. "First she was for Cayo Hueso, then she was dead against it, and then . . ."

"She changed her mind *again?*"

"Yes. The last word I heard was that she again proposed placing the housing development in the salt pond area. However, I don't think any papers have been signed. The second will might have given her lots of trouble."

Katie hid her surprise, realizing that she hadn't read far enough in the news articles. She made a mental note to check them again. And why hadn't Rex mentioned Elizabeth's second change of mind? She tried to recall their dinner conversation. Maybe she hadn't given him time. She was the one who had tried to divert the talk from the murder. If Po was right, there might be complicities involved that could have a bearing on Alexa's murder.

"I've seen politics at work, Po. Many final decisions are based on compromises. I'll delve more deeply into the facts surrounding the Cayo Hueso Project."

"Good idea." Po slouched against the hard back of the chair. Then he leaned forward, pulled a checkbook from his blazer pocket, and wrote Katie a retainer.

"Care to tell me why you consider Elizabeth a suspect?" Katie asked.

Po pocketed the checkbook. "Better talk to Layton about it. That's my advice. She lined up on his side at the start — gung ho for the housing project. To see it a successful actuality would probably have meant a promotion for her — a governor's appointment to a higher paying job, I suppose. You know how that sort of thing works. Honor, glory, and more money plus a step up on the career ladder."

She nodded. "On the Monday of Alexa's death, Elizabeth Wright was against the housing project. Alexa's new will would also have worked against Cayo Hueso. I can't see why or how Alexa's death could have benefited Miss Wright."

"It's a puzzle," Po said.

"But then . . . if Elizabeth finally decided to support the project . . . the situation leaves some questions unanswered."

"I think so. You may find my opinion self serving, but I have a gut feeling that there's something hidden in that Cayo Hueso situation that needs your attention."

"I intend to study the Cayo Hueso development thoroughly."

"Maybe Rex and Liz had a lover's spat that made her threaten to block the project. Maybe Elizabeth held her right to veto over Rex's head as a threat in order to get her own way about something. I can't figure it out. You're the detective. Think about it. That's what I'm paying you for."

"I'll do that. It's a promise."

"A woman scorned may do strange things."

"A woman scorned?"

Po chuckled and looked directly at her for the first time. "Rex's quite a man about town, you know. He and Elizabeth saw a lot of each other for a while. You might want to check into what cooled that romance. When a relationship goes on the rocks, the rocks are usually in the bed. Maybe she changed her mind once too often. Sometimes a man needs to know exactly where he stands with a woman."

"Thanks for the tip." Katie tried to show insouciance toward Rex's love life. She wished she could say his choice of lady friends failed to interest her, but not so. They interested her both personally and professionally.

"Heard you had dinner at Louie's Back Yard last night." Again Po met her gaze.

"Is Bubba working for you, too?" Katie kept her voice light, but she resented Po's intrusion into her private life. Or maybe one had no private life in the pseudo-paradise of this island. She would have to be more discreet.

"No, Bubba isn't working for me. Maybe I should hire him, at that." Po stood, making a big effort to organize his bones into an upright position. "I do want to see Alexa's killer brought to justice."

Katie dropped Po's check into her desk drawer. "I'll do my best to make that a reality. Thanks for stopping by."

Po pulled his cold pipe from his pocket and clamped it between his teeth before leaving the office. Katie stood at the window watching his departure and she was about to return to her desk when she noticed a yellow Volkswagen driving slowly past. A burly man sat at the wheel and his scraggly red hair and full beard held her attention as he stared at the McCartel/Hassworth office. For a moment she thought he was going to stop and park at the curb in the slot marked "clients only," but he drove on. She smiled. The guy had looked like a whale wedged into a sardine can.

Flies had left specks on the window, and

she dampened a paper towel to clean the glass. She had almost forgotten the man in the VW until she noticed him drive past the office again, again peering toward the building. For an instant their glances met, but he looked away quickly as he sped on down the street and out of sight.

She tried to place the man. Had she seen him before? A client? That hair was unique. Surely she would have remembered if they had met before. And the yellow VW? Did she know anyone who drove that kind of car? She shrugged as she dropped the paper towel into the wastebasket. Maybe he was one of Mac's acquaintances, perhaps a chauvinist who would approach the office only if he was sure Mac was in and he wouldn't have to deal with some skirt.

She had work to do, but she stood at the window, waiting, keeping the jute drapery between herself and the glass. She saw the car pass the office two more times before she left to meet Beck for lunch.

Chapter Eleven

It was almost two o'clock when Katie approached the sprawling Queen Anne mansion next door to the Dades' residence. A Conch Train filled with tourists sounded its strident whistle, and Katie pulled over to let the long yellow and black vehicle pass before she parked in front of Beck Dixon's tearoom.

Towers. Bay windows. Dormers. Sculpture columns. Hibiscus House evoked impressions of past grandeur, and as Katie paused at the steps, Beck and the enticing fragrance of Cuban coffee greeted her. Looking like a picture from *Southern Living*, Beck strolled across the wide veranda in a sea-blue jumpsuit, adjusting the pink hibiscus blossom tucked behind her left ear. If such a thing as sleepy alertness existed, Beck Dixon had it.

"Dear child, I hope you can tolerate a late lunch." Beck pulled out white wicker chairs and they settled themselves at a round glass-topped table protected from the wind, where pristine napkins folded into fan shapes surrounded more hibiscus blossoms floating in a milk glass gravy boat. "I wanted to wait until the crowd had thinned so we could talk privately."

"Any time is a good time to be at Hibiscus

House. I've been looking forward to our lunch all morning. It sounds enticing on such a blustery day."

"Crab salad is the specialty of the day."

"Sounds wonderful." Katie felt her mouth watering as a waitress served their salads along with steaming cups of coffee and a basket of warm rolls.

"You're probably wondering why I've invited you here." Beck sipped her coffee then continued. "Diane told me on our early walk this morning that you had agreed to investigate Alexa's murder."

"Right."

"I know dawn can break without my being there to sweep up the pieces, but as I told you the other night, I *want* to help. Maybe if I fill you in on my impressions of the Chitting family, it will benefit you. I've known them for years."

"I'd appreciate your help." Katie felt wary of Beck's eagerness to impart gratuitous information although she had no reason to suspect any ulterior motives. Diane had told her that in the past Beck frequently offered a sympathetic ear but that she seldom offered advice unless asked.

"You haven't asked me where I was the night of the murder."

Katie blinked at Beck's bluntness. "Okay. I'll ask. Where were you?"

"Right here in the tearoom. I played

hostess to an evening meeting of the Preservation Group's Ways and Means committee. I can give you names. Grace Benton. Gladys Southard. Maud Pearlford. They'll all vouch for me."

Katie jotted the names in her notebook. "Thanks. I'll check with them."

Beck changed the subject abruptly. "I've known the Chittings for years, and of course I knew Alexa long before Diane was born. I can give you a fresh perspective. Children sometimes have distorted views of their parents."

"I suppose that's true." Katie added a bit of salt to her salad and waited.

"Alexa and I were childhood friends. She was Alexa Morgan then, but after we left high school, we seldom moved in the same social circles. I earned straight A's all through school, but I couldn't afford college."

"And you wanted to go?"

"Yes, I did. Instead, I settled for taking some correspondence courses in English and business as I made the most of my talent with food. I went to work as a cook at Casa Marina while Alexa flew to attend Vassar."

"What was the source of Alexa's wealth?"

"Alexa's grandfather was a ship's captain — a wrecking captain."

"I understand that the salvaging of wrecked ships was a regulated industry years ago."

"Yes. Between the eighteen-thirties and eighteen-fifties, the population of Key West grew from five hundred souls to twenty-seven hundred, and most of these people were New Englanders or English Bahamians involved in the wrecking business."

"Sounds rotten — people profiting from the misfortune of others."

Beck shrugged. "The law made wrecking a legal business. Millions of dollars worth of salvage cases involving ships wrecked on the reefs went through the Key West courts. The general rule was that the first captain to reach a distressed vessel owned salvage rights to that ship."

"He got everything?"

"Oh, no. The cargo was brought to shore and sold right here on Key West docks. The wrecking captain received a percentage of the sale on everything he and his crew had salvaged."

"Some deal."

"Alexa's grandfather, or maybe great-grandfather, became extremely wealthy from the wrecking business. He also doubled as a minister and when he preached, his wife watched the reef from their widow's walk. There's a story that during one sermon this wife sent a sealed message to her husband telling him that a ship had foundered on the reef."

"I suppose that broke up church for the day."

"Not so. The minister ended his sermon

quickly, gave the benediction to the bowed worshipers as he walked the aisle from pulpit to the rear door of the church, then ran to his ship, getting a head start to the distressed vessel while his parishioners were still saying their Amens."

"It must have been a colorful era."

"From what I've heard and read, it was. The men wore silk top hats and the ladies, dressed in satins and lace, served tea on fine china — even on gold plates." Beck rose, went to a dining room cupboard, and returned with a silver teapot. "This is a piece of salvage rescued by my great-grandfather."

Katie held the heavy pot, admiring its sheen, its intricate design. "I feel as if I'm holding history in my hands."

"It's the only heirloom I have from the salvage days. Through the years, hard times forced my family to sell the other pieces. I've heard there were diamonds and pearls along with a gold-plated coffee pot."

"I suppose the coming of the steamship ended the salvage business." Katie set the teapot aside.

"Yes. That, along with the building of reef lighthouses."

"Did you keep in touch with Alexa after she went to college?"

"Very casually. She'd come home for holidays and for summers, and sometimes we'd get together for lunch or for a sunset picnic on the beach. Alexa enjoyed the Morgan millions and she'd bring college friends to Casa Marina for dinner, always requesting the most expensive dish on the menu — my special crab-stuffed lobster."

"I'm surprised she didn't choose to live in the East," Katie said.

"Some Conchs find it hard to shake the sand from their shoes. Alexa and I loved this island. It didn't surprise me when she chose to live here. She captivated Porter Chitting and brought him with her, and her family set him up in business — Chitting Marina. Of course, it's always been Alexa's money that's kept the enterprise going."

"Nice for Po."

"Maybe. Or maybe it marked his downfall. He had won some literary prizes at Yale." Beck shrugged. "Who knows what might have been? At any rate, I grew tired of cooking at Casa Marina, and when I mentioned it to Alexa she offered to set me up in my own business."

"Just like that — a your-wish-is-my-command sort of thing?"

"Yes. Very much like that. Conchs tend to take care of their own. I snapped up her offer. But the tearoom was no gift. Get that straight. I had inherited this house from my parents, but it took a lot of money to modernize the kitchen and remodel the downstairs to accommodate luncheon guests."

"A grand home like this, yet you couldn't afford college?"

"My dad inherited the house from his father. It was built in the Bahamas, torn apart and shipped here when the focus of the wrecking business shifted to Key West."

"Torn down and shipped?" Katie asked. "Sounds impossible."

"Many houses back then had no nails. Their joints were fitted together. Guess the place came apart like a puzzle and went back together the same way. Granddad was a good businessman, but Dad wasn't. After several unfortunate ventures, the house was all he had. We were a poor family."

"It's a lovely place. Your hard work and impeccable taste have worked together to make the tearoom a success."

"Thank you. It's been my life. And a good life at that. I repaid Alexa every cent — with interest, and nowadays, although I seldom do the cooking anymore, I'm usually still around to play hostess. Alexa always brought her friends and business associates here for lunch. Her support never lagged."

"You knew her well. And you must have liked her."

"Yes. I did like and respect her. Some people called her tough-minded and hard, but she dealt fairly with business associates and with the public. Other people snipped at her morals. I made no judgments."

"Live and let live."

"Right. I never had any problems with her. As we grew older we both began working in the Preservation Group. Neither of us wanted to see Key West develop commercially to the point that it turned into a miniature Miami Beach."

"I can understand that." Katie bit into another roll, enjoying its yeasty warmth, forgetting the calories.

"The news of Alexa's cancer devastated me, but it comforted me to know that she could afford the best doctors available."

"Where did she go?"

"Sloan Kettering, back East. Her illness angered her and she never hesitated to verbalize that anger. She raged. Sometimes I think she blamed her family for her illness, or perhaps resented them for being healthy."

"And she made no secret about changing her will?"

"No secret at all."

"That must have caused a lot of talk around town."

"I'm surprised you didn't hear something of it."

"Wasn't paying attention, I guess. Mac and I've been working very hard to make the agency go. Our work involves some travel at times. Guess our attention was on our clients and our cases."

"I can understand that," Beck said. "That's

why I want to fill you in on the Chitting family. You need to find out what happened on that Monday night, and you need some background details to help you."

"Let's forget the family for a moment. You mentioned Rex Layton as a suspect. How do you read him?"

Beck thought for a moment. "Oh, Rex thinks big. He's never been a detail man, and although he can charm the fish from the sea, he'd have to hire someone else to clean and cook them. He has lots of big plans for Key West including the Cayo Hueso Project, but he needs practical help in implementing those plans."

"He had a lot to lose if Alexa's new will had gone into effect?"

"Dear child, it could have meant his job. He's an elected official, and the business community wants to see Key West expand."

"So if Rex can't bring about that expansion, this bloc of business people may back a candidate who can, right?"

"Right. Expansion means more money for them. I get angry just thinking about some of the things the City Council has allowed to happen to this island."

"I suppose you're thinking about the big cruise ships docking at Mallory."

"I certainly am. For years both the locals and the tourists have enjoyed strolling on the dock at sunset and watching the street performers. You know what's happened to all that. Builders cut the dock in size as they readied it for the cruise ships. Now it's so minuscule that there's barely enough room for the jugglers, the tight-rope walker, the dancers to perform. Many of them have moved elsewhere. The plaza at the Hilton Hotel offers performing space for a few."

"The tourists miss them. I hear talk about that, but at least the cruise ships move during the sunset hours."

"And well they should." Beck's face flushed. "Who wants to see a cruise ship between himself and the sunset! I abhor them, but the business people see only the dollars those cruise passengers pour into the tills."

"So we have cruise ships."

"And we have high-rise condos. The council tried to restrict them to four stories, but the builders and their smart lawyers worked around that limitation by designating the ground level as parking area. They claim the first floor starts above that. Lots of people who once had sea-view homes now have backside-of-the-condo-view homes."

"Do you know Elizabeth Wright?"

"I've met her." Beck sniffed as if she smelled something unpleasant. "Frankly, I don't like her."

"Any special reason?"

"Dear child, surely you've seen the woman! Her and her sexy air of aloof sophistication!

She turns heads or stomachs, depending on whether her audience is male or female."

Katie smiled. "At one time she was in agreement with the mayor about the Cayo Hueso Project being built at the salt pond location. So I'm wondering what changed her mind. Did you and Alexa influence her?"

"Don't think we didn't try." Beck gave a pettish thrust to her lower lip. "At first Rex was more influential with her than we were. He's a charmer, but then Elizabeth changed her mind, refused to sign the necessary papers, and came up with several ideas of why the project should be dropped. Alexa and I cheered her decision."

"Why? I need to know why she changed her mind."

"Maybe you'll have to ask her personally. I don't have the answer."

"And then she changed her mind a second time, again ready to support Cayo Hueso at the salt pond location. Why?"

"Another something to look into, dear child. I said I could tell you about family. I didn't say I could figure out Elizabeth Wright and her motives."

Katie sipped her tea without replying, again wary of Beck's volunteer help. She wanted to ask more about Po, about Mary Bethel, about Randy Dade, but she held back. As if Beck could read her mind, she spoke up.

"Sooner or later you'll hear talk about

Randy. It's not rumor. It's truth."

"And?"

"Not too long ago he flared up at Alexa for trying to persuade Diane to send their kids up north to a private boarding school. Randy said he'd see Alexa dead before he'd let her interfere with his family."

"Did you hear this threat?"

"No, but I know people who did hear it. I never took his words literally. Randy has a temper, but basically, he's easy-going, and I can't imagine him murdering his mother-in-law or anyone else."

"Why are you telling me about this rumor?"

"I wanted you to hear it from me before you heard it from someone else. Try to imagine it, Katie. It must have been hell being Alexa's son-in-law, loving Diane and having to listen to a lot of guff from her mother. For the most part I think Randy handled their relationship very well."

Katie glanced at her watch then scraped her chair back. "Thanks so much for the lovely lunch and for all your help." She rose. "I have another appointment now, and I'll certainly bear in mind all you've told me. I appreciate it, Beck."

"You're welcome, and I wish you all success."

As she left the tearoom, she wished she didn't have the feeling, the hunch, that Beck was spoon-feeding her only what she wanted her to know, that she was holding back important facts. But how could she complain? She was lucky that Beck was willing to give her any information at all. She sat in her convertible jotting notes about the case before she drove back to her office.

The mail had arrived and in it she found a large manila envelope bearing Attorney Addison's return address. She removed photos, looked at them quickly, then slapped them face down on her desk. She read the report carefully, trying not to gag at the graphic descriptions of Alexa's body.

One by one she looked at the grisly photos again. Could that mangled mass of flesh and bone once have been a living, breathing person! She recalled a poster she had hung on her school bulletin board: *Life is fragile. Handle with care.* She shuddered as she reread the police report that mentioned nothing about a bullet hole in the wall hanging. The hole in the black border would have been easy to miss. Even if the police had looked behind the hanging, they would have seen nothing of interest on the wall. She guessed that Alexa's body and all the blood and gore caused by the conch shell attack had distracted the officers. The thought of a gunshot probably never entered their heads.

Chapter Twelve

When Katie left Beck Dixon, the day had grown even more chilly and foreboding. Evidently the weatherman was going to be right about the week-long cold front. She closed her office window against the dank air, then telephoned Mary Bethel. Great luck. Mary was in and she agreed to see Katie immediately. Maybe she was eager to get the questioning behind her.

When Katie arrived, Mary was standing in her office doorway, again wearing black. A slim woman stood talking to her. Thirtyish. Power-dressed for success — if a linen suit, stiletto heels, and a heavy gold chain designated success.

Katie watched the woman adjust the thin strap of her sleek leather bag into a more comfortable position on the shoulder of her chocolate-brown suit. Her dark hair, thick and wedge-cut, contrasted dramatically with her white silk blouse, and when she turned slightly, Katie recognized her. Elizabeth Wright.

"I've come to speak to you about my boat," Elizabeth said, her tone supercilious. "I want to berth it here at the marina for another month."

"You'll have to make arrangements at the dockmaster's office." Mary frowned, her voice as cold and forbidding as the day. "You'll find it downstairs and to the left on the first level."

"But . . ."

"I'm sorry. I can't help you here."

Katie looked at the boats in their slips as if averting her gaze would make her deaf to the conversation, to Mary Bethel's proprietary tone. Elizabeth Wright. Had the murderer returned to the scene of the crime? Katie couldn't imagine so elegant a lady bashing Alexa Chitting with a conch shell. In the next moment the woman departed, her heels clicking as she headed for the stairway.

"Please come in, Miss Hassworth."

Mary Bethel's voice sounded only a few degrees more cordial as Katie turned and entered the office. Again, Mary's black hair and dress contrasting with the white silk walls lent her a fragile silhouette quality. She motioned Katie to a chair and took her usual position behind her walnut desk. A green cursor blinked on the blank computer screen, and Mary typed a staccato command that cleared the monitor.

"How may I help you?"

"By answering a few questions." Katie pulled out her notebook and as she settled into her chair, she felt the leather cushions mold to her hips and back and she welcomed the warmth. "How long will you stay on here, Mary?"

"Until the family asks me to leave. Porter Chitting's in charge now, but . . . well, he's a busy man and there are bills to pay, accounts to keep, queries to answer. And the family owes me employment at least until the end of the month. That's for sure. I depend on that paycheck." She motioned to the computer terminal on her desk. "Of course, I have a lot of free time, too. I write. It's quiet here and I come in early each day. It's a good place to work."

A luxurious place to work. An office a writer might kill for? "When did you find Alexa's body, Miss Bethel?"

"When I came to work last Tuesday morning."

"Where did you find the body?"

"Alexa . . . she . . . it was behind her desk, slumped over the arm of her swivel chair."

Katie saw a slight shudder of revulsion cross Mary's shoulders, but in spite of her hesitations, her voice sounded strong and she continued to meet Katie's gaze.

"Did you think there was a possibility that she might be alive?"

"No."

"Did you touch the body?"

"No. No."

"But you were sure she was dead?"

"Yes. I was sure." Her voice caught and

127

she cleared her throat. "There was so much blood everywhere, and her head . . . her head was too badly . . . mutilated. I knew without a doubt that she was dead."

Now Mary became restive, squirming, licking her lips, twisting her slim fingers. Katie eyed the fingers. They looked too fragile, too well manicured to have wielded a conch shell.

"What did you do after you discovered the body?"

"I called the police."

"Not the ambulance?"

"No." Her voice grew harsh. "I told you. I knew that she was dead. An ambulance crew couldn't have helped her. I called the police."

"Then what did you do?"

"I waited for them to arrive."

Katie noted the sarcasm. "Where did you wait?"

"I stood outside on the balcony. I couldn't bear to stay in the room with . . ."

"I understand. How long did it take the police to arrive?"

Mary thought for a moment. "Five minutes or so, I guess. But that morning, it seemed that it took them forever. Seems to me they *owe* people a quicker response."

"They questioned you, I suppose."

"Yes. Quite thoroughly. I agree with them that Alexa must have surprised a burglar, probably a drug addict. I can't imagine why she didn't fling the money at him and tell him to go."

"He? You feel the murderer was a man?"

"Yes. Yes, of course. I can't imagine a woman doing such a thing or having the strength the attack must have required."

"When was the last time you saw Alexa alive?"

"When I left work on Monday afternoon."

"And what time was that?"

"Around five o'clock. Maybe a little after."

"Was there anything different about that afternoon?"

"Nothing that I remember. I had done some shopping for Alexa. Personal things."

"What sort of personal things?"

"A new nightgown. New panties. Some Shalimar perfume."

"Was there some special occasion in her life?"

"A late evening date, I think. She didn't reveal her plans."

"Did you often do her personal shopping?"

"Yes. Often. I was far more than a secretary to her."

"More like a daughter?"

"I wouldn't say that. No."

"I understand that Alexa and Diane were often at odds. Perhaps she treated you better than a daughter."

"No, not at all."

"Then what did you mean by your comment that you were more than a secretary?"

Mary shrugged. "I merely meant that I did much more for her than take dictation and type letters and keep files straight."

"I see." Katie looked at Mary, saying nothing more. She had learned that trick as a teacher. Her principal had pointed out that few people could tolerate a prolonged silence, that some atavistic need usually prompted speech. She waited.

Again Mary grew restive, and then words came tumbling. "I mean, I'm not complaining about the personal errands I did for Alexa. Don't misunderstand. Alexa paid me well and she allowed me to choose my own hours. All she asked was that I get the marina work done on time. She was a good boss, a true friend, and I hope you can find the person who killed her."

"I'm certainly going to try. Why was it important to you to work, as you say, your own hours?" Katie sensed Mary's slight hesitation.

"I enjoyed the convenience of it. Most bosses expect an employee to punch the time clock. Alexa was different. If I didn't feel like coming until ten o'clock, that suited her. No problem. She paid for work completed rather than for the number of hours expended."

"You like to sleep late in the mornings?" Again Katie sensed a hesitation in reply.

"No. I get up around six to write. I liked to do my own work in the quiet of early morning while my mind is fresh and before I came to the office."

"When was the last time you saw Alexa alive?"

"I already told you. I last saw her a week ago Monday when I left here for the day around five o'clock."

"Tell me about that time."

"There's nothing special to tell. I finished three or four letters and placed them on her desk for her signature. I knew she probably wouldn't sign them immediately. She usually reread letters and signed them the following morning. Sometimes she changed her mind about mailing them."

"A sound practice," Katie said. "But go on. What else did you do before you left for the day?"

"Nothing. I just slipped on my sweater and walked out the door. Alexa called goodbye, and I returned her farewell. There was nothing special about the moment."

"Did you go straight home?"

"Yes."

"And you stayed at home all evening?"

"Yes. I have a neighbor who can vouch for that. Maria Gonzales."

"You talked to this neighbor that night?"

"No. But Maria's the curious kind who keeps tabs on the neighborhood. She's innocuous. You know the sort. Elderly. Little to do to occupy herself. She usually knows what's going on in the houses around hers."

"She's snoopy?"

"No. Just interested. And aware. She's a good kind of neighbor to have. She told the police that she heard my radio that night and that she saw me sitting at my desk. In fact she had a guest that evening. Rosa Abresco. They both saw me — heard my radio."

"Is that possible?"

"Of course. My desk sits by the window. My landlady's Italian and she's strong for cooking with garlic, so I keep my window open a crack to let in fresh air even on chilly nights. I also keep my shade drawn, but the ladies could see my shadow. They knew I was home."

"You were writing that night?"

"Yes. I'm a free-lance writer. Articles, mostly."

"The radio doesn't distract you?"

"No. I tune in an FM station that plays classics. The music masks other noises that might be a distraction."

"Where have you been published?"

Mary opened a desk drawer and pulled out a thick scrapbook, which she shoved across the desk toward Katie. "Here's some of my work. I'm no wishful tyro. I've sold to lots of national newspapers and magazines."

Katie turned the scrapbook pages, pausing to read two short articles in their entirety. Lucid writing. Strong leads. Good middles.

Strong endings that harked back to the leads, giving the reader the satisfying feeling of having come full circle. Mary's writing showed a competent journalist at work. Katie could identify with her. They both enjoyed words.

"Nice articles, Mary. You must have worked hard to accumulate so many published credits."

"Right. I have worked hard. Writing requires lots of time and quiet concentration. I try to keep no less than a dozen submissions in the mail."

"Now you have more time for your work."

"Yes. I have lots more time and now I do most of my writing here. I enjoy using the word processor."

"What time do you arrive at the office?"

"Usually before seven. That gives me a couple of uninterrupted hours before the phone starts ringing."

"Did you ever work at the office at night?"

"Sometimes, but not often. If Alexa had extra work for me, I might return at night and do it because that would free my morning for my own writing."

"Alexa was generous to you in her will."

Mary straightened in her chair, then leaned forward. "That's true. But if you think I killed her for financial gain you're mistaken. I'm a thrifty person. I manage nicely on my salary and the checks for my writing."

Katie stood. "Thank you for your time. Your answers have facilitated my investigation."

As she left the office, Katie sensed Mary's shrewd gaze boring into her back. She didn't turn, but she knew Mary watched her until she was out of sight. *Little Mary Bethel.* Somehow Po's diminutive didn't quite fit, and her own comparison of Mary to a fragile silhouette now seemed flawed. Determined. That was the only word for any free-lancer who rose at six to write, who kept a dozen submissions circulating at all times.

Chapter Thirteen

Late Tuesday afternoon, Katie delivered the Lowery report as Mac had requested, then she wrote three dun letters that would go out in Wednesday morning's mail. In a cash flow emergency she could draw on the Chitting retainer, but she preferred to wait until she had finished her investigation before touching the Chitting money. Mac would have had no such qualms. She sighed. Maybe if she solved the Chitting case before Mac returned, it would bolster her confidence. She reached for the telephone.

Setting up interviews just minutes before her arrival gave a suspect less time to prepare answers. However, she knew Po Chitting had probably been polishing his alibi ever since Mary Bethel had discovered Alexa's body.

So, back to the marina. She parked in a visitor's slot then hunched her shoulders against the dank fish-scented wind as she walked toward the dockmaster's office. Near the planked walkway, three gulls fluttered and screamed, fighting over a foul-smelling scrap of squid a captain had tossed from his yacht.

"I have an appointment with Porter Chitting," Katie announced, standing just inside the dockmaster's doorway. "Could you direct me to his office?"

A young dockmaster wearing the Chitting uniform and logo smiled and rose from his desk. "Yes, Ma'am. I'm going that way. Just follow me."

Their steps echoed against concrete in the lower level of a parking ramp before they reached a spacious, high-ceilinged shed that housed new boats, motors, and a repair shop. The smell of fresh paint and diesel fuel permeated the area as someone revved a motor. Startled, Katie almost slipped as she sidestepped a small pool of spilled oil.

"There's Po's office, Ma'am." The dockmaster nodded to a closed door at the rear of the shed. "Just knock. He's in there."

She approached the door and gave three hard raps.

"Come in."

Opening the door, she stepped inside the office, where her nose caught the smell of dank plaster as her eyes adjusted to the dim light that slanted from three high windows. Po's furniture consisted of a scarred desk, a couple of oak chairs, and a small bookcase with a broken bottom shelf. The only bright spot in the room was a lighted aquarium where tiny fish darted among floating water plants. By comparison, this room made the McCartel/Hassworth office seem plush.

With a cold pipe clamped between his

teeth, Po slouched in one corner, winding line on a fishing reel. Pausing, he wiped one hand on his chinos then pushed up the sleeve of his black turtleneck.

"Give me a hand, will you?" His violet-colored eyes were dark with concentration.

"Certainly. What's to do?"

"Grab that spool of line and steady it."

Katie picked up the spool, holding it in her cupped hand as the line played from it.

"Promised both grandkids new reels for our fishing trip next week. They've got a contest going. Trying to see who'll catch the first sailfish. I spoil them with reels and lures instead of ice cream and candy."

"Does Diane object?"

"Nope. Never has. At eight and ten, they're great kids. They keep me young." He finished winding the line and took the empty spool from her. "Thanks. You saved me some serious grief."

Po laid the reel on his desk, motioned her to a seat beside the aquarium, then dropped into his swivel chair as if gravity had conquered all his muscles. On his disheveled desk, file folders and old newspapers mounded in stacks that threatened to *glissando* to the floor. Beck had been wrong about a word processor. Nothing that modern graced the office. She eyed a sheet of yellowed paper protruding from an ancient Royal sitting on a typewriter table at one side of Po's chair.

"Tell me about your aquarium." She watched the colorful fish swimming in the huge tank.

"It's a salt water set-up." Po laid his cold pipe aside. "Lex and Tracy are helping me monitor it and catch suitable specimens. There's a lot of mathematical detail involved in maintaining the correct water temperature, salt concentration, oxygen level. I like to see the grands learning some math skills on a practical level as they enjoy working with the fish and the tank. But you didn't come here to discuss aquariums. Let's get to business." He clamped the pipe between his teeth again.

"I understand you're a writer."

"Correct. Been working on a novel for some time now. It's coming along fine. I just need to do a bit more background research before I can finish it."

"Will this be your first book?"

Po turned and pulled a thin volume from his bookcase. "Years ago when I was in college, the university press published this volume of my short stories. It won the Remington Literary Award. The honor carried no monetary value, but I basked in lots of honor and glory."

"They must be good stories. I did some writing while I worked on my master's degree. But I never won an award." She took the book, opened it, and ran her forefinger down the table of contents. "Sea tales. Interesting."

"The grandkids love them. When they stay

overnight at our house, they get bedtime pirate yarns instead of fairytales." Po chuckled as if the thought gave him pleasure. "Some of the stories are true, too. Key West has a fascinating history. I had visited the islands and studied them many years before I met Alexa. My parents came here on holidays when I was a kid."

Katie returned the book to him. "Po, when did you learn about Alexa's death?"

"The police brought the news to my door a little after nine o'clock in the morning one week ago today. Tuesday."

She could tell the question wearied him. And he'd probably be tired of the others, too. But she had to ask. "Were you surprised by the news?"

He looked at her, startled. "Why, of course. I could hardly take in what they were saying. I rushed to the marina and to Alexa's office immediately."

"You hadn't realized that she had been absent from home all night?"

"No. We live in a spacious house. It's no big secret that we go our own ways. I was unaware of her absence."

Suddenly she felt sorry for two people caught in such a perfidious relationship. Her voice softened. "When did you last see Alexa alive?"

"On Monday morning. I saw her twice that Monday. We had breakfast together at home, then she stopped here at my office later in the morning."

"Was that her usual habit?"

"Not necessarily. But sometimes she would stop by or maybe I'd go to her office. It all depended on circumstances."

"What were the circumstances that brought her here that last Monday?"

"She wanted to discuss her new will and she was also talking about applying to take an experimental drug that some doctors believed might help lung cancer patients."

"How did you feel about this?"

"The medicine? I was all for it. What she needed more than anything else was hope."

"I notice that you smoke a pipe."

"*Smoked* a pipe, I've been trying to stop ever since we learned of her cancer. Figured I might be next."

"The will — let's discuss that."

Po shrugged and dropped the pipe into his desk drawer. "I really doubted that she'd carry out her threat to sign the new will. Alexa's always been headstrong. Understandably, she was upset and angry at this time, but I had talked with her doctor and he had told me that anger was a phase terminal patients went through before they accepted their situation. I didn't believe Alexa would vent her anger on her family by leaving everything to the Preservation Group."

"When was she scheduled to sign the new will?"

"The next day. She had an early-morning appointment with Sam Addison on Tuesday."

"Were you the only one who knew this?"

"No. The whole family knew it. Little Mary Bethel knew it. Business associates at the marina knew it. Alexa made no attempt at secrecy. I think she enjoyed the attention."

"Anyone else beside close associates know about the will?"

"Town gossips spread the word here and there. I heard innuendoes in the bars. Where there's money, there's talk. Someone acted before the deadline."

Would Tyler Parish have known the time of the new signing? Katie refrained from asking that question. "Then you doubt the robbery theory?"

"Right. I do. A robber would have used a gun, not a conch shell. And a person who had planned a robbery would have made certain that he had taken all the money available."

"How much money did he overlook?"

"Over three hundred dollars. Not a lot to some people, but megabucks to a hophead. No. I'll always believe someone planned the robbery as a sham."

"What would you have done had the new will been implemented?"

Suddenly Po suffered a paroxysm of coughing. When he recovered, he flushed and slouched more deeply into his chair. "You mean how would I survive without Alexa's

141

money? Frankly, I don't know." He stared at the aquarium. "It might have forced me to get a job, to do something worthwhile for a change."

"Perhaps you would have finished your book."

"Perhaps. But the sale of a novel by an unknown writer seldom puts much bread of his table. Oh, I had a big motive for killing Alexa. Perhaps several motives. But the fact remains, I didn't do it. And I want you to find out who did."

"Police found a button from your jacket near Alexa's body." She let the statement hang between them, listening to the aquarium filter bubble in the silence until he responded.

"Yes. That's true. That morning when Alexa and I had breakfast, she saw the button dangling from my sleeve and she pulled it off. I hadn't noticed it, but there was another button missing, too. I'd bought the jacket in Rome, and the buttons were distinctive. Alexa kept the button she'd removed and said she'd see about ordering replacements."

Katie nodded. "Po, who do you think might be guilty?"

"Someone who profited by her will, of course. To my way of thinking, it's just a matter of finding out whom. That's your job." He chuckled.

"Something's funny?"

"Yes. Definitely funny. Here I am *paying* you to ask me questions that could land me in jail — or worse."

"Where were you on the Monday night a week ago?"

"At Captain Tony's Saloon. Lots of friends can vouch for that."

"Do you spend many evenings there?"

"I spend most of my evenings out — usually at a bar. Sloppy Joe's. Two Friends. Pier House. But on that Monday I hung out at Captain Tony's because he has a fireplace. A cold front passed through on that night, and lots of locals and tourists warmed their buns around Tony's hearth."

"You say you've friends who can vouch for your presence?"

"Right. There's Jib Persky, for one. The bartender. He knows I was there and I think he'll remember the night because the day had been so hot. Why, I'd taken my grandkids swimming at Smathers Beach that afternoon. Jib will remember the day — and the night."

"What makes you so sure?"

"Because he usually has to hire extra help when a real norther hits and the thin blooded locals head for Tony's."

"Who else will remember your presence at the bar that night?"

"Dwight Chalmers. Red Worthington. Spike Daters. They're all steadies."

"And they were all there the whole evening?"

143

"Well, they were there a good part of the evening. I left around midnight."

"Then the only person who was there the whole time you were there was the bartender, Jib Persky."

"I guess that's right. You talk to him. He'll back me up."

"Thank you for your time, Po." She rose. "I'll keep in touch."

"Katie?" Po remained seated.

She paused, sensing a new intimacy in his tone. "Yes?"

"There's something you need to know."

"There's a lot I need to know." She sat back down, waiting.

Po folded his arms on the edge of his desk and leaned forward. "On the Friday before her death, Alexa withdrew a hundred thousand dollars from her bank account."

"A hundred thou!"

"Right. In cash. Nobody knows where it went — where it is."

"Who else is aware of this?"

"Diane. Randy. Addison. The bank."

"Mary Bethel?"

"We don't know. If she knew about it, she never mentioned it."

"Why didn't someone tell me sooner?" She felt her face grow hot, but she controlled her anger. "If I'm to investigate for you, you're going to have to level with me — about everything."

"We talked it over — Diane, Randy, and I. We were trying to be discreet. We thought whoever had the money might accidentally reveal himself if nobody was nosing around, putting him on guard. But now I think it's time you knew this — for all it's worth."

"Have you checked at the local banks to see if anyone made a big deposit?"

"I know the bank presidents and I've checked with them. They have to report large deposits to the IRS. They say there were none."

"Could she have hidden the money some-where?"

"I suppose so. But where? And why? Think about it." They both stood and Po walked her to the door.

Katie returned to her office, her mind a muddle. A hundred thou withdrawn from Alexa's account and she was just now finding out about it! How could she solve a murder if she didn't have all the facts? What else was the family keeping from her?

Where was that hundred thou now?

The fact that a neighbor saw a shadow and heard a radio playing wasn't enough to free Mary Bethel from suspicion, nor did Po's alibi carry much weight. Of course, maybe he talked the whole evening with Jib Persky. That was possible, but not probable.

Could Bubba have been mistaken about

seeing Po that night on Houseboat Row? She also thought of Rex's alibi, knowing she would have to talk to Attorney Addison again. The missing hundred thousand added a new dimension to the case. It was time to do some in-depth checking on alibis. But not today.

Chapter Fourteen

Katie returned to her office to jot more comments on the Chitting case, to review the notes from the previous two days, to think about the facts she had gleaned. About five o'clock she made out her day's time sheet, then telephoned Samuel Addison.

"Yes, Miss Hassworth?"

"Rex Layton says he presided at the city council meeting the night Alexa Chitting was killed. True?"

"Yes, indeed. Rex presided."

"And he never left the council room?"

"Not until the meeting adjourned around eleven o'clock."

"Diane was present all evening, too?"

"Correct."

"Thank you, sir."

"You're welcome. Call again if I can help."

It surprised her to realize how pleased she was to know that Rex had an irrefutable alibi, but she deplored her lack of insight concerning the killer's identity and hoped she hadn't overlooked some obvious clue that would have led a more experienced detective straight to the murderer's door.

At five-thirty she entered the front of the

Dade mansion as Randy slammed into the kitchen. Lex and Tracy left the family room TV to rush to the kitchen and give their dad a hug.

Katie smiled at Randy as they met near the stairway in the foyer. "Good day on the flats?"

"A grand slam day. Tarpon. Permit. Bonefish. The big three." He grinned and polished his blackened piece of eight against his sweatshirt in a child-like tribute to his good luck.

"Will you join us for supper?" Diane stepped through the kitchen doorway. "Conch chowder, salad and garlic bread. I've made enough for everyone and I'd like to hear how you're coming with the case."

"Thanks for the invite, but no. I've questioned lots of people today and I really need quiet time to consider and reconsider their answers. Raincheck?"

"Sure."

Katie looked back at Randy. "Since fishing's so good, could I book a day?"

"Gotcha." He tightened the leather thong holding his hair off his shoulders. "When'll it be?"

"How about day after tomorrow?"

"Thursday?" He shook his head. "Look, I know you need to question me about Alexa, but you needn't buy a day on the *Lady Di*. Want to rap after dinner?"

"Thanks, but I really do need some

thinking and note-jotting time before I make more queries. And I'd enjoy a day's fishing. Or even a half-day if you're pushed for time. Are you booked all day Thursday?"

"Yep. Sorry. A regular customer comes down on that date every year. It's his birthday. He thinks it's lucky."

"And is it?"

"Sometimes. But he's a good fisherman. The good ones make their own luck. How about tomorrow? It's supposed to be cloudy and cool, but no wind. I could take you out in the morning if you really want to go."

"Deal. Could we make it a half day?"

"Gotcha."

"Diane, how about coming along? I'll pack a lunch and we'll make an outing of it."

"Sounds good. Haven't been out on my namesake in ages."

"We'll cast off from the Stock Island Marina around eight," Randy said. "But I'll have to leave here about seven-thirty. You can ride to the marina with me if you don't mind waiting while I rig up."

"Fine," Katie said. "No use taking up two parking slots in that crowded area." She wondered if Randy would patronize the Chitting Marina in the future, now that Alexa was dead.

"If we catch grouper, I'll cook them for our dinner," Diane said.

"I only promise fishing," Randy said. "No

promises at all about catching."

Katie trudged to her apartment, feeling envious of the Dades' family life and wondering how her own marriage could have turned into such a fiasco. She made her supper, keeping it well balanced, holding down the calorie count. Plain yogurt. Banana and kiwi salad. Skim milk. Appropriate fare for the gourmet-ascetic. She sighed and tried to avoid thinking of the garlic bread and chowder Diane was serving downstairs.

After she finished eating she showered and climbed into bed, propping herself against her pillows as she studied her notebook. Once again she listed the suspects she had questioned, along with their alibis. Diane had attended the city council meeting and she had lots of witnesses, including Samuel Addison and Rex Layton. She drew lines through those three names.

Mary Bethel claimed neighbors would vouch that she had been home. But had she? Po claimed he had been at Captain Tony's. But had he? All evening? Maybe she shouldn't have booked tomorrow morning on the *Lady Di.* Maybe she should have used the time to check on alibis. But she could do that in the afternoon. She needed to talk to Randy, to hear his story about his mother-in-law's murder.

Wednesday morning dawned calm, cloudy, and chilly, and she dressed in layers she could peel off in case the sun appeared later. Shorts under jeans. Tank top under turtleneck under sweatshirt. She packed ham and cheese sandwiches, chips, sodas, trying to ignore the fat content. Neither Randy nor Diane were calorie counting types. Before leaving her apartment, she grabbed a fishing hat, sunglasses, and sunscreen. And her notebook. Once outside, she wished the world had a remote control that allowed people to fast-forward gloom to sunshine.

Randy wore only khaki shorts, shirt, and a blue windbreaker, but Diane was layered much the same as Katie. They drove toward Stock Island, nosing into the traffic on Eaton Street then making a sharp left turn onto North Roosevelt and crossing the Boca Chica Bridge. At the marina parking lot, low, gray-blue clouds pushed the stench of gasoline, oil, and fish close to the ground. Boat captains and fishermen hurried about, shoulders hunched, necks drawn turtle-like into their jackets and sweatshirts.

Katie and Diane waited in the dimly lit dive shop, showing superficial interest in treble hooks and tube lures. They studied a display case of shiny doubloons and encrusted pieces of eight which Mel Fisher had traded the shop owner years ago for some of the diving gear necessary to continue his search for the *Atocha*.

"Let's go, women," Randy called at last.

151

Katie followed Diane to the dock, waiting until Diane took her hand before she stepped onto the teakwood gunnel and then down into Randy's seventeen-foot backwater boat. She eased past fishing rods standing at attention in the rack by the console and sat on the fishing seat, scooting over to make room for Diane. Randy stowed their lunch in an ice bin under the poling platform at the stern.

"The *Lady Di*," Katie said. "Nice name."

"Named after my Di, not the British princess." Randy grinned at his wife. "But the name draws attention and that's good for business. Potential customers notice it and it sticks in their memories." He started the motor and eased the *Lady Di* from the marina, leaving no wake. When they reached the channel, he increased their speed, heading under the bridge and toward the Gulf. "What would you like to fish for today?"

A murderer. "How about 'cuda?" Katie asked. "Would we have any luck at that?"

"Maybe." They took a long fast run over cobalt waves before he cut the motor, hoisted himself onto the stern platform, and poled the *Lady Di* into shallow water so clear and still it might have been an illusion. "Stand on the bow, Katie. Diane, you can cast from the stern. Try not to tangle your lines, ladies."

"I'll just watch today," Diane said. "Have at it, Katie."

"I've spotted one to the starboard." Randy pointed. "See it? Quick! Make a long cast. Two o'clock."

Katie looked, saw nothing, but made the cast, dubiously watching the pink lure splash into the sea. "Did I come close?"

"Pull it in. Fast!" Diane said. "Wind it!"

She cranked, feeling the vibration of the reel and hearing its clicking sound.

"Too late," Randy called. "You got to plunk it right in front of his nose. He's still cold and sluggish." He poled for a few more minutes, then he turned the boat slightly to port side. "There. See that dark spot on the white sand at eleven o'clock. Throw! Now!"

This time she saw the fish, cast toward it, and began reeling.

"He's eyeballing it." Diane hopped onto the fishing seat for a better view.

"He's following it," Randy said. "Jiggle your rod. Good. Now reel. He wants it. Here he comes!"

She felt the 'cuda hit the lure and she reeled frenetically, forcing the rod tip up, letting the fish take line, then reeling it in again.

"He's coming in," Diane shouted.

"Keep the rod tip up!" Randy yelled. "Let him have some line. Now reel! Watch it. He's going under the boat."

"If he heads for the prop . . ." Diane broke off mid-sentence.

Katie stepped down from the bow and stood on the port side, reeling, reeling. The 'cuda swam in front of the bow once more, a silver streak against the dull gray-green of the turtle grass, and she cranked the reel faster, feeling her arm muscles begin to ache, her fingers grow numb.

"He's coming close. He's tired." Randy knelt at the starboard side with a gaff, ready to boat fish. "Want to keep him?"

"No point in that. Release him, okay?" She fought to keep the rod tip up.

"I want to see him," Diane said. "I brought my camera."

"Gotcha!" Using the gaff, Randy brought the 'cuda aboard. His biceps bulged as he held it up. "He'll go thirty pounds at least. Maybe more."

Diane snapped three shots, and Katie noted Randy's strong hands and arms as she marveled at the weight and length of the fish that reached from his chest to the deck. Then she nodded. "Put him back."

Randy lowered the 'cuda into the sea, carefully removing the gaff and gripping the fish by the tail. He eased it back and forth through the water until its strength returned, then it lunged from his grasp, swimming across the crystal flat and disappearing into the blue water of the channel.

"Nice catch," Randy said. "Want to try for another?"

"Let's talk. My arms need a rest." She sat on the bow, facing the wheel. "I do need to ask some questions." Both she and Diane refused the soda Randy offered, and he began drinking it.

"I realize I'm a suspect," Randy said. "But I think my alibi will satisfy you."

"And I'll vouch for him," Diane said.

"Okay. Let's hear it. Where were you on that Monday night?"

"I drove to Big Pine Key to attend a fly tying session at a friend's house. He has a shed on his property where we can spread out our stuff without driving his wife crazy. There were eight or ten of us present that night. I can supply names. The guys will back me up. We meet once a month and I'm a regular."

"What time did the meeting break up?"

"At nine o'clock. Big Pine's a thirty to forty-five minute drive from Key West, depending on traffic."

"The med examiner set the time of death between eight and ten," Diane reminded her.

"I know," Katie said.

"Under usual circumstances I would have been home a little before ten, but that night slow drivers clogged the highway. As you know, there are few places to pass. And then, three cars piled up on the Niles Channel Bridge."

"How bad?"

"No one seriously hurt, just shaken up, but the incident caused a real traffic tangle. One of the cars flooded and wouldn't start. It was blocking both bridge lanes and everyone had to wait it out."

"Did anyone call the police?"

"A patrolman stopped and helped get traffic moving. Took him about an hour."

"So what time did you get back to Key West?"

"It was well after ten. Close to ten-forty-five. Right, Diane?"

"Right. I was clock watching. That highway's a bear, especially at night when the drunks and druggies feel compelled to get behind the wheel. I always worry when Randy doesn't come in on time."

Would she lie for Randy? Protect her husband at all costs? Katie doubted that. Diane had been a straight arrow in all their dealings. She'd check on the accident. That should be easily verified. Bridge accidents were common. The locals accepted such delays with equanimity. The tourists were the ones who got uptight and loud-mouthed and sometimes obstreperous.

"Randy, there's a rumor that you threatened Alexa's life. True?"

Randy peered at the horizon, then his blue eyes narrowed as he met Katie's gaze. "Alexa and I had lots of arguments, and I'll admit I said I'd see her dead before I'd let her interfere with my marriage or my family. I didn't mean it literally." He paused again. "At least I don't think I did."

"Of course you didn't," Diane said.

"Alexa offered Diane money to pay tuition for the kids at a private eastern boarding school. I let her know I wasn't having any of that shit."

"And you blurted the threat in anger?" Katie asked.

"Right. Alexa really riled my plumbing. She had a million ways of letting me know I was trash, that I wasn't good enough for Diane or the Chitting family, wasn't good enough or smart enough to raise my own kids."

"I won't deny that," Diane said. "Mother's attitude toward Randy was one of the main reasons she and I grew apart."

"That must have been hard to take," Katie said.

"Right." Randy scowled. "Alexa steamed me. When we were first married I made the mistake of borrowing money from her for a down payment on our house. I paid it back on time and with interest as we had agreed. I repaid the *money,* but I could never repay the *debt.* Alexa was forever reminding me of the time she helped me out when I was down."

"So you didn't get along with your mother-in-law and her acerbic tongue. That's understandable." Katie studied the waves for a few moments, then she looked directly at Randy.

"Who do you think might have killed Alexa?"

"I don't know. It could have been any of the suspects we discussed the other night. She was a bitch. Don't know how she could have raised such a great daughter."

"That happens sometimes."

"Don't know how Po stood her all those years. Maybe he finally got fed up with being a doormat. Nobody'd blame him. Then there's Tyler Parish. Maybe he got a belly full of the gigolo scene."

"Randy!"

"I heard his paintings were beginning to rate national acclaim," Katie said.

Diane nodded. "Yes. He was developing a distinctive style and becoming more than just another painter of seascapes for the tourists."

"Maybe he saw a way of making it on his own," Randy said. "And maybe she wouldn't let him go."

"I've thought of some of those things, too," Katie said. "I haven't questioned Parish yet, but I will. And I still need to talk with Elizabeth Wright. Either of you know anything about her?"

"A career-oriented woman on her way up," Diane said.

"At least that's the talk around town," Randy agreed. "Rex plays the field, but the two of them seemed pretty close for a while."

"What happened?" She tried to keep her tone professional, and she saw Diane lean forward with interest as Randy spoke.

"Don't know what cooled them off. Maybe she found someone else. Or maybe he did." Randy mounted the poling platform once more and scanned the sea. "How about some more fishing? The wind's coming up and in a few minutes the tide will be right on another flat near Old Man Key. Some big ones usually hang out there."

"Then let's go check it out."

"Gotcha."

Chapter Fifteen

On Wednesday afternoon, Katie talked with Grace Benton, who confirmed Beck Dixon's presence at Hibiscus House at the time of Alexa's murder. Next she called Maria Gonzales, and a half-hour later she stood on the porch of Maria's weathered Conch house across the street from Mary Bethel's second floor apartment. Katie looked down at the squat old Cuban. Wiry. Ferret-eyed. Suspicious. She was like a wrinkled crab ready to attack or retreat, depending on situational demands. As she smoothed a spotless white apron over her red gingham dress, a chill afternoon wind tossed her golden hoop earrings. She began twisting her wedding band.

"Please to meet my friend, Rosa Abresco," Maria said. "She is here to confirm my true words to you."

"Good afternoon, Mrs. Abresco." Like Maria, Rosa was short. She had a determined set to her jaw, and she wore mourning from her babushka to her flat-heeled shoes that poked from beneath her long skirt. Her doleful costume suited the gloomy day.

"Buenas tardes, Senorita." Katie smiled, hoping Maria would invite them inside where it was warmer.

"Please to sit down." Seeking a wind-sheltered spot, Maria pulled forward a wicker chair that had lost its battle with dank air and mildew, then she and Rosa sat in similar chairs and faced their guest. "Questions you have?"

"Yes, Mrs. Gonzales. As I told you over the telephone, I've been hired by the Chitting family to investigate Alexa Chitting's death."

"Is too bad, the passing of the grand señora. But I know nothing of it. I am one who minds her own business."

"Sí," Rosa said. "Likewise myself."

"I've come to ask you about Mary Bethel who lives in the apartment across the street. I understand you've already talked with the police concerning Mary's whereabouts on the Monday night of the murder."

"Yes," Maria said. "To the police I tell all I know. And there you have it."

"Please repeat your story once more, Mrs. Gonzales. Did you see Mary Bethel on that Monday night?"

"Yes. I am not nosey. But one can not help seeing what is directly before one's eyes. Is right?"

"Of course. And you saw Miss Bethel too, Mrs. Abresco?"

"Sí. Is like Maria says. Sí."

"You're both certain you saw Mary Bethel the night Mrs. Chitting died?"

161

"Because this is my house and I sit here often whether it be hot or whether it be cold. I did see Mary Bethel that night. And I hear her radio playing that night. The sound, it carry clearly on this quiet street."

"It carry," Rosa echoed.

"I understand the weather had turned cold that Monday. Much like today." Katie shivered. "You ladies didn't mind the chill while sitting on your porch?"

"No," Rosa said. "I tell you. We no mind."

"I am tough old bird." Pride tinged Maria's voice. "Twenty years ago I escape to this island on a raft. I survive. Ninety miles of open sea. Now I do not let weather dictate to me. Free country. Not like Cuba. I sit where I want to sit. I sit when I want to sit. If it be cold, I wear a shawl."

"I see." Katie felt admiration for the resolute old lady. "Did Mary usually play her radio at night?"

"Sometimes yes. Sometimes no. But on that night you speak of, she played it."

"Sí," Rosa said.

"Music?"

"Usually she play music. But that night, no. No music. What you call a talk show. Man. Woman. Jabbering."

"No comprende." Rosa nodded.

"I see. And you saw Mary that night?"
Both women nodded.

"Yes," Maria said. "This Mary Bethel, she

writes. Her desk, her writing machine sit directly behind first window on the right."

Maria pointed. Rosa nodded.

"That night the window shade was pulled to the sill," Rosa said. "That was her usual habit."

"We see her shadow against the shade," Maria said. "She sat at her machine all the evening until she turn out light a little after eleven o'clock."

"Is correct." Rosa tightened the knot on her babushka.

"You're sure of the time?"

"Sí."

"Yes. Eleven o'clock news come on. Light go off."

"If the shade was drawn to the sill, how can you be sure it was Mary Bethel sitting at the typewriter?"

Maria Gonzales grinned, revealing a missing tooth and three gold caps. "I know the person is Mary Bethel from shape of head. Mary Bethel wears wig."

Rosa giggled. "She bald. At night she — what you say relax — take off the wig."

"Uncomfortable," Maria said. "Hot. Itch. Easy to see her head's melon shadow shape against the window shade."

"I see." Katie smiled and rose, surprised to learn of Mary Bethel's baldness, but never doubting Maria's words. "Thank you, Mrs. Gonzales, Mrs. Abresco. You've been a help and I appreciate your talking with me."

"You welcome. Any more you want to know you come to Maria Gonzales." Both Cuban ladies stood.

"Thank you again for your time."

Katie left the women and drove one block to Fleming Street, parking in front of the library. A wig. She hadn't guessed, although she had noticed Mary's every-hair-in-place appearance. Now she remembered Samuel Addison's words about Mary suffering from a high fever. Mentally she marked Alexa's secretary off the suspect list. That made four people in the clear — Diane, Beck Dixon, Rex, and Mary. And it narrowed the list to Po, Randy, Elizabeth Wright, and Tyler Parish. Still a long ways to go, but maybe she could cross Randy and Po off the list once she checked their alibis. Maybe Bubba had been wrong about the time he had seen Po on Houseboat Row. How much credibility could she put in a druggie's word? Or a bartender's?

As usual the library felt hot and stuffy. A sign warned patrons that the uniformed guard sitting at the entry had the right to check all bags, but this morning *Time* magazine held his attention. Katie requested copies of the *Key West Citizen* dating from the day of the murder to the present, and after a short wait, a page supplied them. As Katie carried the papers to a table for perusal, she guessed that the three street people dozing nearby contributed directly to the room's gymnasium smell, but she hadn't the heart to complain and have someone ask them to leave. She couldn't imagine what it would be like to be homeless.

She searched the papers for an article concerning a wreck on the Niles Channel Bridge, but found none. Strange. If Randy had been lying, he was a smooth prevaricator. As she checked all columns again, the rustling of the paper awakened one of the dozers. He glared at her, then nodded off again. Katie rose. Why would a bridge accident have gone unreported? An oversight? A mishap too slight to rate ink? None of the above?

She returned the papers to the main desk and left the library. The guard never looked up. Cushy job.

It was three-thirty when she drove to the police station, circling the block twice before she was lucky enough to find a parking place. She sat in her car thinking. Afraid? She tried to tell herself she was just nervous. Why was she doing this? Mac had taught her early on that private detectives frequently provided information for the police. But the police seldom reciprocated. Leaving her car reluctantly, she walked slowly, hesitating before the low building that seemed to be crouching, waiting.

Stepping inside, she saw a gray haze of smoke hanging near the ceiling. Maybe ceiling smoke filled a requirement of all police stations. A slight, blue-uniformed cop stood behind a pine desk, his brown cigarette dangling from the corner of his mouth and adding to the air pollution. Her shoes scraped against the tile floor and she cleared her throat.

"May I help you?" The cop sized her up, his dour expression unchanging.

Sgt. Babcock. She read his nametag. "I'd like to see the officer in charge of the Alexa Chitting murder, please."

He picked up a phone, muttered a few words, then looked up. "Lt. Brewer will see you. Down the hall to your left. First door."

Katie found the office and paused in the doorway. From behind a gray steel desk, a stocky middle-aged man with porcine features stared up at her without rising. Wrinkles creased his brown suit, a loosened tie hung at his throat, and a wilted collar gave his white shirt the appearance of having been slept in. Even if pungent gray smoke hadn't been rising from the black cigar clamped between his yellowed teeth, his low forehead would have called attention to his snout-like nose and mouth.

"Lt. Brewer here," he grunted. "What do you want?" He laid the cigar aside, letting it smolder.

"I'm Katie Hassworth." She opened her billfold and flashed her identification. When he nodded, she continued. "The Chitting family has hired me to investigate Alexa Chitting's death. They don't buy the robbery theory."

"Too bad. The case's still open, but we're not discussing it with the public."

"I'm investigating Mrs. Chitting's close associates and their motives. I'd like to see the murder weapon — the conch shell."

His piggy eyes roved over her body. "No doubt you've looked over Florida laws regulating the activities of private eyes. Under no circumstances will this department tolerate infringement by private investigators, even blonde types with green eyes and legs as long as the Alaska pipeline. The murder weapon is unavailable to you."

She had guessed that the shell would be unavailable. She also knew he was trying to bait her with his sexist remarks and she ignored them. An argument would get her nowhere. "There are several people right in this city who had plenty of motive to kill Alexa Chitting."

"I'm aware of that. All cops aren't dumb, you know. Who's rating your special attention? Po? Parish? Or Randy Dade? Which one?"

"I'm here to check on an accident that stopped traffic on Highway One on the night of the murder."

"Don't know of any such accident."

She sensed a chink in Brewer's macho armor, something in the way his voice dropped in volume yet rose in pitch as he quickly picked up his cigar, inhaled deeply, then looked out the window. Porky Pig was lying.

"Niles Channel Bridge, Lt. Brewer. I understand the traffic snarl lasted about an hour."

Brewer rose and crossed to a steel file cabinet, shuffled through some manila folders, then returned to his desk shaking his head. "Got no accident report for that night, but I wouldn't show it to you if I did have."

"An accident on that bridge would have been reported here, wouldn't it?"

"It most certainly would. What makes you think someone crashed that night?"

She hesitated, squelching an urge to tell the police nothing. "Randy Dade says he didn't get home until well after ten o'clock the night of the murder because a wreck tied up traffic at Niles Channel. He said there were no personal injuries and he also said that a patrolman stopped and helped untangle the mess and get traffic moving again. I looked in the newspaper and found nothing about an accident. Thought maybe the report failed to reach the paper."

"No report because no such accident happened at that time or place."

Katie felt a twinge of guilt over what she was about to say concerning Diane's husband, but the words had to be said to help complete her investigation. "Then maybe you'll want to check on Randy Dade's alibi yourself. He had motive to kill his mother-in-law. If he wasn't delayed on the bridge, he had opportunity. And from what you're telling me, it appears that he's lied about his movements on that night."

"Look lady, we don't have unlimited manpower here. With the drug situation raging, it takes all the cops we can muster just to keep the streets safe for decent humanity. If I go investigating Randy Dade, or any others of the multitudes I've already talked to and who had motive and opportunity to off Alexa Chitting, I'd need to add extra staff and pay the regulars overtime. Got no money for such luxuries. You've gotta understand. We're doing all we can." He jumped up and stepped around to her side of the desk, dribbling cigar ash down his shirtfront.

"And no doubt the solving of this case will make your name an eponym in South Florida if not throughout the state." Katie turned before he could step any closer to her. "Thank you for your time, Lt. Brewer."

She left his office and the police station, wondering what it was between the police and private investigators that brought out the worst in both. Egos got in the way. The police hated losing face when someone solved a case outside the department. And private investigators? Brewer was right. She wasn't working for free. If the ingenious police solved every case, she and Mac would be out of business. She grinned. The threat was minuscule. She consoled herself by remembering that the P.I's and the police had one important thing in common. At some time in their lives they both had decided to be on the side of the good guys.

Katie drove to the beach, parked across from the Key West By the Sea condos and set out on foot, scanning the crowd of afternoon sunbathers. Bubba saw her before she saw him and joined her, approaching from behind.

"Bubba! You startled me." She eyed his filthy cutoffs, the only clothing he wore. Had he sent everything to the laundry? She corked a smile. Today his hair had escaped its leather thong and it straggled heavy and matted around his tanned shoulders.

"Private eyes startle easy." He swiped the back of his hand across his nose as he sniffled. "What's new?"

"I might ask you the same thing. Anything to report?"

"No."

"Want to work?"

"No. But I will. Haven't eaten since yesterday."

"That means you've skipped brunch, right?"

"A guy needs breakfast. And lunch. Most

important meals of the day. That's what they told me in reform school."

"I can't imagine that you progressed as far as reform school."

"You're wrong. I got there all right. I had the aptitude for it, but I was a reform school dropout. They may still be looking for me in Rhode Island. What's the job?"

"One important thing. I want to know if there was a wreck on the Niles Channel Bridge on the night of Alexa's murder. I found nothing in the newspaper about it. Police say they have no record of it."

"So why do you think it happened?"

"Randy Dade says it did. I believe him. Anyway, I want to believe him."

"Okay. What else?"

"Nothing else. One thing at a time, please."

"Will do. Any advance money?"

"None. But the minute you produce, I'll pay."

"Friendship means nothing to you?"

"Friendship means everything to me. That's why I pay only on receipt of information. Keeps my friendships intact."

"You're a hard woman, Blondie." Bubba turned on his bare heel, heading in the opposite direction, and she walked on for five minutes before returning to her car.

Three years ago, had anyone told her she would one day be dealing with the Bubbas of the world, she would have called them crazy.

Chapter Sixteen

Katie gave herself a few more minutes to cool down after talking with Lt. Brewer before she walked to Capt. Tony's in Old Town. A Beatles' rendition of "Hey Jude" blared from the jukebox in the hole-in-the-wall saloon that opened right on a level with the sidewalk, and she found herself inside its dim interior almost before she realized it. She stood for a moment beside the oval-shaped bar. Once her ears adjusted to the high decibels and her eyes to the low light, she noticed a yellow cat sleeping on the barstool next to her. To her right, a lounge area centered on a smoke-blackened fireplace, and the whole saloon was a perfumery of whiskey, spilled beer, and cigarette smoke.

The place was deserted except for the yellow cat, an old Conch drinking beer at the far end of the oval, and the middle-aged bartender, a short and fat man wearing barkeep chic — faded tank top, frayed jeans, dirty Nikes. He reminded her of a bloated elf.

"May I help you, Ma'am?" The elf decorously swiped a gray rag across the bar, leaving a damp streak in its wake.

She eyed a barstool bearing the name

Spike painted in bold black letters and she raised her voice above the cacophony of the jukebox. "This seat reserved?"

"Not at the moment. Spike won't show until after six. Enjoy."

The Beatles tune ended, and she basked in the sudden silence. The cat lifted its head and twitched its tail as if the quiet had disturbed its sleep.

"Do you serve sandwiches?"

"No food. Just drink."

"I'd like a beer, then. Light, please."

He uncapped a Miller's and set it and a glass in front of her. His bored expression and slow quiet movements gave her the impression that a trained ape could handle his job with no sweat. But under his sleepy lids, she discerned bright sparrow-like eyes covertly studying her.

"Are you Jib Persky?"

"The same."

"Katie Hassworth, private detective." She pulled out her billfold and flashed her license, which he barely gave a glance. "I'm investigating the Chitting murder and I'd like to ask some questions."

"You going to read me my rights first?"

She smiled. "That's police procedure. My questions are informal and they concern the whereabouts of Porter Chitting on the night of his wife's murder. That was a week ago this past Monday. Mr. Chitting says he was here and that you can vouch for that. True?"

"He was here. I've already told the police that. I remember the date because it had been hot as Hades all day, then a cold front blew in about eight o'clock. Capt. Tony lit some logs in the fireplace and the bar filled up fast. The locals rate cold right along with AIDS and heart attacks. I had to call in a buddy to help me keep up with business."

"And Mr. Chitting came in at what time?"

"He came in shortly after seven o'clock and he took his usual place."

"Which is where?"

"Sixth stool down from where you're sitting."

She read the barkeep well. He not only knew the score, but he also knew the full names of all the players without having to check his program. She slid off her stool and walked to the seat Jib indicated. The letters PO were painted on it.

"Everyone has his special place?"

"Just the regulars. And the cat. Jezebel outranks a tourist any night of the week." With studied nonchalance Jib picked up a dingy towel and began polishing bar glasses. She returned to the stool marked Spike and wondered if he had touched the glass she was using with that towel.

"And Mr. Chitting remained here all evening that night?"

"As far as I remember, he did. I don't recall him leaving until around midnight."

"Did he always stay that late?"

"That was his usual custom, but sometimes he left earlier or sometimes he didn't show at all."

"But on that Monday he stayed until midnight."

"Yes."

"Could he have slipped out unnoticed? Left for half an hour or so and then returned?"

"I suppose that's possible, Ma'am. What with drinking and all, most guys go back to the biffy to take a leak now and then." He nodded toward the restroom at the back of the bar. "I don't make them sign up for the privilege."

"You're saying that Mr. Chitting could have left for a short time and returned to his barstool without being noticed."

"That's possible. All I can tell you for sure is that he was here that night and that I didn't notice him leaving until around midnight. On other nights he'd sometimes slip out for a couple of hours to visit Angie, but not that night. She works on Mondays. Po was here."

"Angie? Who's Angie?"

Jib Persky gave his full attention to rearranging his bar paraphernalia. For a few moments she thought he was trying to recall Angie's last name, then it became evident that he had turned off his charisma and was merely ignoring her question.

"Thank you, Mr. Persky." She stood, leaving her beer barely touched. "You've been helpful."

Squinting against lambent sunshine that was fighting a losing battle with the clouds, she strolled back to her office, thinking about Jib Persky and Po. Since the bar had been crowded that Monday night, Po could have slipped away unnoticed. He could have walked the few blocks to the marina, killed Alexa, then reclaimed his barstool as if he were returning from the john. Somehow she doubted that he had done that. Bubba claimed to have seen him on Houseboat Row. Would a stoic who had endured Alexa's domineering for years suddenly take action in his own behalf? Maybe. Maybe he would if he saw his opulent lifestyle threatened. She sighed. She couldn't cross Po off her suspect list just yet.

On impulse she decided to visit Tyler Parish's place of business — the artists' studio a couple of blocks from the sea on Simonton Street. Parish didn't know her. She could browse as a tourist or an art lover with no need to make her professional presence known. Maybe seeing some of his work would give her some clues to the inner man.

HAVEN OF THE ARTS. She read the words on the pink and gold sign under an apricot tree which shaded the two-story building that had been turned into an artists' workshop. Diane had told her the place was a draw, that many tourists enjoyed watching artists at work. As she entered, the premises weren't crowded, but there were a few people milling about. Good. She didn't want to be conspicuous.

"May I help you, miss?" A blue-smocked woman rose from her easel, smiling.

"I've just come in to look, thank you." She peered at the street scene in progress on the easel. "Lovely. Are you painting it from memory?"

"No." The woman pointed to a small photograph at the side of the easel. "It's a street in Key Largo. I used to live there as a child. I'm Beth Greenwheel. You're free to look around and if I can help you, let me know. I believe the other artists are out right now, but if you have questions, I'll try to find some answers. The others should be returning within just a few minutes."

"Thank you." She started to say that she was interested in Tyler Parish's work, but thought better of it. Did artists suffer from professional jealousy? She was glad Parish was out at the moment.

"Francine Wong's space is right in back of mine," Beth Greenwheel said. "And you'll find Tyler Parish's studio up the stairway at the back. I think he's at East Martello preparing for his show."

Katie glanced at the stairway at the rear of

the building just as a burly man came down the steps and disappeared through a rear door. She stepped behind a large oil, waiting to see if he would return, but she heard a car start. The yellow VW? She recognized him as the one who had circled her office the day Po Chitting had called on her. When she felt sure the man wasn't coming back, she pretended to look at more paintings for a few minutes, then she left the building without venturing to the second floor.

Unnerved. That's how she felt. Had the man followed her here, slipping in the back entry as she went in the front? Maybe he had been following her all afternoon and she'd been too careless to notice. Or maybe she was getting paranoid. Who was that man? Maybe he was an undercover cop checking up on her private investigation. But probably not. Even a cop would have been subtler. At any rate, she'd had enough of the art studio for now. She probably shouldn't have come here. Parish had said he would call her after Thursday. She should give him the courtesy of waiting. Plenty of time to tackle him later, if his call didn't come as promised. Somehow she guessed that it wouldn't.

Her telephone was ringing as she entered her office and she made a dash for it.

"Hassworth and McCartel."

"Thought it was McCartel and Hassworth," Rex said.

"Only when McCartel's in town." She laughed, pleased to hear Rex's voice. Subconsciously, did she want to be the head of the agency? Unlikely!

"May I take you to dinner tonight? I hear there's a new chef at Sugarloaf Lodge."

"That sounds very inviting. What time?"

"Around five-thirty. Okay? Hope that won't rush you."

"That's early, but I can make it. I'll be looking forward to it."

"And so will I. See you then."

She sat down still staring at the telephone, but as she tried to concentrate on Jib Persky, Po Chitting, and the man at the art studio, her mind kept dwelling on Rex. She wasn't ready for a new relationship. Not now. Maybe never. Then she laughed. What was wrong with her? Rex had asked her to dinner, not to bed. She started to smile at her foolishness, then she stiffened. An almost imperceptible sound put her on guard. When she looked toward the door, Bubba was leaning against the jamb watching her.

"I didn't hear you come in." Although nothing minatory showed in his manner, she had to struggle to keep her voice casual but firm.

"Bare feet give advantage." Bubba sniffled and approached her desk.

"You might consider knocking. People do it every day."

"I found out about that bridge wreck."

"Quick work. Then there was one? Niles Channel?"

"Right. It didn't make the rag or the police blotter. They hushed it up."

"Who hushed it up?"

"Brewer. The looie."

"Why?"

"The deal was to find out if there was a wreck. More info costs you more bread."

"Okay. Another ten. Why did Brewer hush up the wreck?"

"The accident involved his kid. He was drunk again. It was about his umpteenth offense, and in addition to the rotten publicity for the kid, his family, and the police force, it would have meant a suspended license." Bubba held out a grimy hand. "Payday?"

Katie pulled a twenty and a ten from her billfold and laid them on her desk, watched him scoop them up and stuff them into his pocket.

"Thanks a bunch. The bucks will brighten my evening." He turned and headed for the door.

"I've another job for you."

He stopped and faced her again. "Too much wealth may corrupt me."

"Risk it, okay? I need to know who Angie is."

"Angie who?"

"That's what I want to know. Angie who?

An Angie who's a friend of Po Chitting's. See what you can find out. I'd like her last name and her address."

"That'll cost you another twenty." He watched her reaction. "Hope you ain't got a cash flow problem."

"Okay. Twenty."

"Let's see your money."

"You mean you know who she is?"

"Sure. Little Angel. Of course, that's just a nickname. Angie Garcia. She works at Rico's — a bar on Stock Island near the old dog track. The guys that hang out at Rico's kid her a lot about her rich boyfriend."

"Where does she live? Stock Island?"

"No. She's got a floating palace over on Houseboat Row. The drab brown one that's supposed to look like a Swiss chalet."

"You know about Swiss chalets?"

"I been around, Blondie. Don't let my looks and my naïve manner deceive you."

Katie laid another twenty on his palm. "Thanks, Bubba. You save me a lot of leg work."

Bubba grinned, pocketed the bill, and left the office. Maybe she'd made a mistake paying him so much at once. He wouldn't want to work again until he was broke. But he'd be back eventually. The Bubbas of the world always returned.

Angie Garcia. If Po had a girlfriend, then the all-knowing Beck Dixon must have been

181

aware of it. Why hadn't she mentioned Angie when they had talked over lunch? Maybe Beck was trying to help, or maybe she was trying to point the investigation in the direction she wanted it to go. Angie Garcia. She didn't need another name on her suspect list.

Katie locked her office and headed for Hibiscus House.

Chapter Seventeen

Hibiscus House looked deserted. Someone had drawn the window shades and closed the front door, but when Katie knocked, she heard footsteps approaching.

"Dear child!" For a moment Beck looked nonplused, then she smiled and flung open the door. "Good to see you. Come right in."

Katie stepped inside, noting a faint fragrance of cinnamon rolls. Beck led her to an alcove on their right where white rattan chairs with jewel-toned cushions flanked a white-bricked fireplace. In the murky late afternoon light, Beck's jumpsuit reminded Katie of apricots drenched in cream, and the older woman carefully chose a green-cushioned chair. Surely she planned for effect. Katie sat across from her, feeling drab and sparrow-like in her utilitarian chinos and shirt as her fingers rested on the smooth silk of the cushion.

"Something exciting has developed on the case?" Beck leaned forward.

"Yes." Katie decided to drive right to the point, and she looked directly into Beck's guileless blue eyes. "I've just learned that for years Po Chitting has been seeing a mistress named Angie Garcia."

The silence between them sizzled like a fire-cracker on a long fuse. Katie waited. In the distance, a whistle blast announced the cruise ship's imminent departure from Mallory Dock. Closer by she heard the Dade kids playing in their backyard and the strident voice of a tour guide as the Conch Train rounded the corner. At last Beck spoke.

"Yes. Po does see Angie Garcia."

"My knowledge of that fact might be important to the investigation."

"Yes. I suppose it might. But I hope not."

"And that's why you withheld this information?"

"Yes." Beck looked at her left toe. "I had hoped we could keep Angie's name out of this."

"She's a special friend of yours?"

"In a way, yes. I've known her for years. Angie's a spitfire, but she's a good person and she's not promiscuous. She's not brilliant, either." Beck chuckled. "A brilliant woman wouldn't take up with Po Chitting, but Angie's a nice hard-working lady and she comes from a good Cuban family."

"So that makes her above anything as gross as murder and that's why you avoided mentioning her to me the other day?"

"Well . . . yes. Angie's special. She supports herself. She's not a kept woman. Sometimes she waits tables here at Hibiscus House, and she always manages to help me out in an emergency. She's my *friend*, Katie."

"I can understand why you like her."

"A few years ago she even worked for no pay during a spell when I was having tax troubles. She's no killer. Some things a person knows, and I know Angie's no killer."

"How long have she and Po been a two-some?"

"For many years. Angie's a beauty. She could have had lots of boyfriends. She could have married years ago, but for some reason she prefers Po."

"Sometimes a person seeks the safety of dating someone who's legally unattainable."

Beck shrugged. "Really now, must you drag Angie into this investigation?"

"I'll need to talk with her. Frankly, you disappointed me by withholding this information."

"Makes you wonder what else I'm holding back?"

"Something like that, yes. Is there other information you should tell me?" Again she forced Beck to meet her gaze.

"No. Nothing."

Katie looked away first. "You say Angie supports herself, but if Po was a widower, they might marry. Right?"

"I suppose that's possible, but it's only a speculation. As you suggest, perhaps she's afraid of marriage. And given his past experiences with wedded bliss, Po might have some reservations about it, too."

"But if Angie did marry Po, Alexa's new

will could have made a big difference in their future. Few women would rush to the altar to assume the support of a man who has never made an effort to support himself."

"Po writes."

"Yes. That's what I mean. Po writes." Katie stood. "Thanks for talking with me." She turned to leave.

"Dear child, I hope you'll do what you can to protect Angie's name. I didn't intend to be devious. It's just that she's my friend. In my opinion, you'll be wasting your time by focusing attention on her."

"I'll remember that. An investigator's never out to hurt people."

Leaving Hibiscus House, Katie crossed the lawn to the Dade home, called a greeting to Diane, then took the steps to her quarters two at a time and began dressing for dinner. Five-thirty! Why so early? She thought Rex would be more the late-romantic-dinner type. Last time they had dined at seven. This had been her day of surprises.

She showered, checked her weight, then dressed carefully in a creamy knit shift that flattered her figure. Once she was ready, she went downstairs and sat on the veranda thinking about Po Chitting and Angie Garcia until Rex arrived. How unfair for one man to be so handsome! White slacks seemed to be Rex's trademark. She couldn't remember seeing him in anything else. Tonight a black silk shirt accentuated his tan.

"Katie! How lovely you are. I've been looking forward to this evening."

"For all of an hour?" She laughed.

"Glad you could accept on the spur of the minute. I like my friends to be flexible."

Friends? Girlfriends? She wondered how many other numbers he had dialed before trying hers, and she let his comment pass as he helped her into the Corvette, left Old Town, and headed north. It was good to forget the Chitting case for awhile.

"Thought we'd try to reach Sugarloaf Lodge in time for the porpoise show."

"I thought that had been canceled permanently. Someone complained about animal abuse."

"You're right. I had forgotten. But we'll enjoy a good meal. I've heard the chef is excellent."

They drove through irksome going-home traffic for several minutes before they arrived at mile marker 17 and the Sugarloaf Lodge. Katie noted a sign that pointed toward an airstrip, but closer at hand she saw tennis courts, a swimming pool, a small marina. Rex parked near the restaurant then came around to help her from the car.

Sure enough. No dolphin show. He twined his fingers through hers as they followed a path to the restaurant. The waitress led Rex to a table by the window where they had a view of palm trees and green lawn.

"Fish and roast beef are the specialties of the house," Rex said. "Would you like to share a seafood platter for two?"

"Sounds good." She looked at the décor that seemed to run to the greens and silvers indigenous to the ocean. Glancing at seascapes that hung on almost every wall, she wondered if Tyler Parish had painted any of them. The restaurant was a restful place and she relaxed as they waited for their meal until she remembered her last dinner with Rex, remembered how she had dominated the conversation. Maybe tonight she could make amends.

"Tell me about yourself, Rex. How did you happen to move to Key West?"

"It's not all that interesting a story."

"Try me. Stop only if I yawn."

"Touché." He grinned at her. "I'm just in the area playing mayor."

"Before that? Where did you live? Where did you grow up? What was your family like?"

Rex sighed, yet Katie sensed that he enjoyed talking about himself. Didn't everyone?

"I grew up in an old mansion near Hastings on Hudson, New York. It's the silver spoon story."

"Lucky for you."

"Maybe. I attended the proper schools, graduated with a law degree and no sense of where I wanted to go or what I wanted to do or be."

"Many people with law degrees become lawyers."

"My dad mentioned that. Several times. Mother mentioned it also. The idea scared me to death, so I joined the Peace Corps and fled to Africa."

"Of course Africa didn't scare you to death."

"You should understand that. It's similar to your fleeing the classroom for a job as a private detective."

"You've made your point."

"I went truly wanting to help the down-trodden masses in third-world countries, but I hated Africa. Filth. Squalor. Poverty. I could see the overall picture, the whole problem, as clearly as if it were framed and hanging on the wall. I offered some great ideas for helping those people and for up-grading their communities, but no. Nobody, American or African, would listen to me."

"Maybe you tried to move too quickly."

"Right. I should have made haste slowly."

She smiled.

"What amuses you?"

"Your oxymoron. When I taught school, I kept a notebook listing figures of speech that used contradictory terms."

"Such as?"

She thought for a moment. "Such as a cruel kindness or an enthusiastic dislike."

"Then how about government efficiency or army intelligence?"

"You're poking fun."

"Would I do that?" Rex grinned at her.

"I've learned a new word, Miss Hassworth. If I use some oxymorons correctly in my term paper, will I get extra credit?"

"Depends on your choices, of course. Now go on with your story. I didn't mean to interrupt."

"I filed away my grandiose dreams for Africa and spent my two years teaching the natives to boil their drinking water and plow a straight furrow."

"Farmer Layton. I can't quite imagine it."

"Nor could I, so when my stint was up, I went home. Dad owns a chain of hotels and he persuaded me to handle the legal details of the family business. First on his agenda was coming to Key West and buying a hotel to add to the Layton chain."

"Which one did you buy?"

"Dad's first choice was Casa Marina, but buy a hotel? I couldn't even reserve a room in one. They were booked full and it wasn't even the peak tourist season. I finally found a rental room in Old Town and moved in."

"Picturesque Old Town. I'll bet you fell in love with the city and decided to live here permanently."

"Something like that, but it happened gradually. Juanita Montez was my landlady until she bounced me."

"Behind on your rent?" Katie smiled. "Or did she get you for insubordination?"

"Neither. Developers were building a new store at Searstown, and Juanita's carpenter brothers arrived to work on the project. They brought wives and children. Mrs. Montez needed my room for family, so I bought a house."

"Wow! A property owner — just like that."

"I'll say, wow! Even Dad blinked when he heard the price. He blinked again when I bought the two houses adjacent to mine as rental units so I could convert the three back yards into one personal tropical garden big enough for a few palms, a pool, and some patio furniture."

"I haven't yawned yet."

"Then as I began to restore the house, I started reading Key West history. That's when I fell in love with the island and decided to stay. Dad hired another lawyer to work with the Layton hotels, and I became involved in local politics."

"Fascinating."

Their dinners arrived and Rex helped her to some shrimp and a piece of blackened grouper.

She inhaled deeply. "The seafood looks and smells delicious. I could eat the pattern off my plate, but please don't let me do it."

"Enjoy! And stop worrying about your weight. You have a perfect figure."

"Flattery will get you everywhere. I have to watch the calories, though. I used to be a real fatty."

"Can't imagine that."

"After I married I developed a full-blown

case of gormandizing."

"Marriage. Another bit of your hidden past? Again, it's my turn not to yawn."

She wondered if her failed marriage made a difference to him. "Married and divorced. My ex-husband, Chuck Gross, is a clothing designer in New York. Ladies' wear. He spent five years telling me how fat I was, then he ran off to France with a model. At the time, I thought I loved him. I almost stopped eating permanently."

"You still carry a torch for this guy?"

"No. He's out of my life and my mind."

"And heart?"

"And heart."

Suddenly she wondered why she was revealing all this. It certainly would do nothing to enhance her in Rex's memory. But did she want to be enhanced? She did want him to know about Chuck. Best to keep everything in the open.

"Fat or thin, I'm glad you're here." Rex reached for her hand.

"So am I. But nobody comes to the Keys accidentally, do they?"

"That's a question?"

"I mean, tourists might come here on a whim, but it seems to me that real people who land here are either looking for something or running away from something. Sometimes it's hard to tell the difference."

"Ah, a philosopher. It's an idea to think

about. Few of the city's present citizens were actually born here."

She smiled and they spoke little as they finished their seafood platter, topping it off with an orange ice for dessert.

"What a lovely meal! I thoroughly enjoyed it."

"I did too, but the evening isn't over. I have something else to show you."

"What?"

"Come with me. It's a surprise."

They strolled to the Corvette, and Rex eased into the highway traffic, then took a sharp right turn onto a dark and deserted road. Immediately she felt on guard. After a short distance he braked the car, helped her out.

"There it is." He gestured upward with a flourish.

"What is it?" Katie peered through cloud-shrouded moonlight at a brown shingled tower that rose about thirty-five feet above the ground.

"It's a bat tower."

"Can we climb up into it?"

"No. There's no ladder. It's only accessible to bats, but I do think the builder planned to add a means of human access, had his plans worked out."

Katie stared up. "I've always wanted to see a bat tower, although not very much."

"Don't poke fun. Some years ago a Dr.

Campbell from San Antonio believed that bats, not dogs, were man's best friends not only because they ate mosquitoes, but also because their excrement made great fertilizer. He intended this tower to be a condo for bats."

"Truly fascinating." She giggled.

"At one time yellow fever and malaria plagued the Keys. Researchers traced the source of the fever to mosquitoes. This tower was part of Dr. Campbell's plan to eradicate mosquitoes by having the bats eat them. I admire his humanitarian ideas."

"But his plan failed?"

"Unfortunately, yes. But I think it's an interesting story." He took her hand as they walked back toward the car.

Neither of them spoke on the short ride to Key West. Rex turned on South Roosevelt and parked at the White Street pier.

"Think they'll ever repair this place?" Katie eyed the barricade across the entry to the pier and read the warning sign. "Pedestrians enter at your own risk."

"Feel like taking the risk?" Rex opened the car door.

"Why not?" Katie laughed. "Only a few months ago I was driving on the thing. It seemed safe enough then."

Rex pulled a couple of sweaters from the back seat, helped her into one, and put on the other one before he took her hand. She smelled his musky scent clinging to the sweater as they squeezed through the barricade and faced into the salty onshore breeze. He put his arm around her waist, pulling her close as they walked the block or so to the end of the pier where the sea foamed and crashed, sometimes splashing over the pier wall onto the asphalt.

"Are you cold?" he asked.

"No. I love the brisk air. It cleans the cobwebs from my mind."

"Didn't know you were plagued by cobwebs." He grinned down at her and pulled her closer as they leaned against the rough coral of the pier wall.

"Rex! I saw something jump out there. Big! Silvery!"

Rex looked where she pointed. "Probably a tarpon. They hang out around here at night."

"Who could blame them. It's so lovely." She watched a ragged scrap of white cloud drift across the moon and heard the faraway call of a night bird.

The breeze shifted, carrying the scent of jasmine from some distant garden as Rex cupped her face in his hands, looking directly into her eyes. Then he kissed her forehead, her eyelids, her cheeks.

"You're teasing me," she murmured.

"And it's unfair to tease, isn't it?" His lips met hers in a warm kiss that sent delicious shivers through her body. She closed her eyes, enjoying his nearness as they kissed again before she pulled away.

"Ah, Katie." He started to pull her close again, but just then a wave crashed over the wall, drenching them. They both jumped back, laughing. "Some end to a romantic evening." He mopped at his slacks while she slicked her dripping hair back from her face.

"Perhaps the sea is trying to tell us something," she said.

"I don't like its message." Rex took her hand and they jogged to the car, shed their wet sweaters and headed home. Rex Layton puzzled her, and he attracted her more than she liked to admit. But what kind of a man was he? Poor little rich boy who voluntarily served his stint in the filth of Africa? Poor little rich boy who bought three houses in order to have his own tropical garden with a pool? Poor little rich boy who liked to visit bat towers and to kiss his women on an off-limits pier?

"Remember our second kiss, honey? We were drenched on that abandoned pier?"

"People are only supposed to remember first kisses, not second ones," she replied.

Katie laughed at the imaginary conversation.

"What's funny?" Rex asked.

She took his free hand. "Nothing. You. Me. Us. I can't explain it." And she didn't want to try. She disliked admitting she had been moved by their evening together.

Chapter Eighteen

Katie punched her pillow as she awakened at dawn. She had slept fitfully, half rousing many times, remembering Rex's kiss, the bat tower, the pier, the kiss. It had been ages since any man had caused her such a restless night. It had been even longer since she had called a man at sunrise, but she reached for the bedside phone.

"Rex Layton speaking."

"You sound surprisingly alert, and I have a favor to ask."

"Katie? Is that you?"

"None other. I was afraid I'd wake you."

"An hour ago you might have. But I'm an early riser."

"Me too. Early morning's my favorite time. The day's fresh and anything might happen."

"I can't resist a lead like that. What's the favor?"

"You said to call on you if you could help with the Chitting case."

"Right. What can I do?"

"This morning I've an appointment with Elizabeth Wright. Before we meet, I'd like to see the salt ponds that are causing the ruckus between the commercial sector and the Preservation Group. Would you have time to give me a quick tour?"

"I'd love to. In fact, I'll be near your place shortly to check on a reported case of tree abuse. Can you be ready in fifteen minutes?"

"Tree abuse? Not child abuse? Not drug abuse?"

"You got it the first time. Tree abuse. We'll check it out, then we'll drive to the salt ponds."

"I'll be ready. And thanks." She replaced the receiver, feeling euphoric. Fifteen minutes. She dressed quickly, ate her usual light breakfast, then hurried to the veranda as Rex was easing the Corvette to the curb.

"Good timing." She opened the door and slid into the bucket seat.

He covered her hand with his. "Good to see you. I dreamed about you all night."

She wished she believed him. "It was a wonderful evening. I enjoyed it, bat tower, drenching and all." She removed her hand from his. "Now where is this abused tree and why are you checking on it?"

"It's a few blocks from here, and I'm checking on it because the city Tree Commission received a report from a neighbor that some guy is using it as a utility pole. In Key West, that's illegal. Unless he's exonerated, he'll face a stiff fine."

"What kind of a tree is it?"

"Sabal palm."

"They're special? They sprout twenty-dollar bills instead of leaves?"

"You can tease, but the Sabal palm is protected by law. It's been the official state tree for over thirty-five years. It's a shopping center specimen, a median strip regular, and the darling of homeowners."

"You could probably get a job doing PR for the Chamber of Commerce."

Rex stopped the Corvette in front of a small frame house where wires, almost hidden by fan-shaped fronds, had been nailed to the trunk of the palm. "There's my proof."

"What will you do about it?"

Pulling out a camera, Rex snapped several shots of the tree and the house, then they drove on. "I'll see that the head of the Tree Commission informs the home owner that he's violating the law and that the city council has proof." Rex patted his camera. "He'll be asked to remove the wires and he'll probably comply with the request. Most offenders usually do. But enough about palm trees. Onward to the salt ponds."

"Where are they?"

"Near the airport runway. There are about forty-three acres that once were used in the process of making salt by solar evaporation. In the early eighteen hundreds, a thousand people worked there."

"What did they do? Sounds as if the sun

did most of the work."

"Men placed pans measuring about a hundred feet by fifty feet in shallow ponds separated by coral rock walls. They regulated the flow of seawater into the pans, and after that water evaporated, they removed and bagged the salt residue. I understand it was back-breaking work."

"And the industry thrived?"

"It prospered until Civil War times. Key West was the only Southern city under Federal control. The government closed the ponds because the salt was being used to preserve fish that fed Confederate forces."

"And the Preservation Group considers these ponds a historic landmark."

"Right." Rex drove down Flagler Avenue and nodded toward a church. "That church, these homes, the high school — all of them stand on former salt pond land. The preservationists see it all disappearing if they don't put a stop to the encroachment." Turning off Flagler, he parked. "Here we are."

Katie looked at the unkempt land overgrown with tropical vegetation and strewn with trash. "It looks like nothing to me. Zilch."

"Agreed. It contains lots of abandoned military junk, jettisoned furniture, and even some dangerous electrical transformers."

"But look!" She pointed. "There's an egret."

Taking her hand, Rex pulled her to their left. "I see another bird. Look behind that huge cactus and the palm. A great blue heron, I think."

"Right. Isn't it a beauty! I can understand why the Preservation Group wants to save this natural environment. Can't you?"

Rex shook his head. "Not really. This land's an eyesore. It'd take months of work and some megabucks to shape it into anything worthy of notice."

"Yes. Megabucks, I suppose." She studied Rex. "You puzzle me. You're a history buff who finds things like bat towers and salt ponds fascinating. You're an environmentalist who works to save Sabal palms. Yet, you're willing to use this historic wildlife refuge for a housing development."

"I enjoy history and the environment, but my stint in the Peace Corps makes me place people at the top of my list of priorities. Humans may be the most endangered species of all."

"And some are more endangered than others. Alexa Chitting, for instance."

"That wasn't exactly the kind of endangerment I meant."

"I know. There are many dangers in this world."

"The Africans ignored me, but they helped me develop a sense of community. I may be able to make a difference here."

"Those Africans may still be plowing straight furrows and boiling their drinking water — all because of your patient and competent direction."

"Let's hope so." Rex laughed and squeezed her hand as they headed back to the car. "When I moved here, I felt the housing shortage. If Key West is to thrive as anything other than a theme park for the wealthy, the average-income and low-income families must be able to find affordable housing."

Rex started the Corvette. "May I take you to breakfast?"

"Thanks, but I've already eaten. I need to get my car and head to the office."

"The interview with Elizabeth is first on your agenda?"

"Right. Any advice?"

"None. You're on your own." Rex drove in silence for several blocks. "I suppose you've heard that Elizabeth and I have . . . once saw a lot of each other."

"I've heard that mentioned." She grinned at him.

"But that scene's all over. Finished. Done."

"You needn't explain."

"You explained about your ex."

"Nobody could really explain Chuck Gross."

"Nor Elizabeth. Let me say that we broke up when I realized she was using me and my position as mayor to foster her career, then let's relegate both Elizabeth and Chuck to our distant pasts."

"Done!"

"I'd like to take you to dinner tonight."

"You're trying to send me back to Overeaters Anonymous." She smiled, hoping to hide her eagerness.

"I'm not trying to send you anywhere. I want to spend the evening with you. Ah, Katie! You're so easy to be with. Are you busy tonight?"

"No. I'd love having dinner with you."

"Great. Tonight's the opening of Tyler Parish's one-man show at the East Martello Gallery. Have you talked with him yet?"

"No. I called him, but he put me off until after this opening." She didn't tell him about visiting his studio.

"Then let's take in his show tonight. His paintings may give you insight into the man."

"Do you know him?"

"By sight and rumor. He has quite a reputation around town — artistic and otherwise."

"I suppose I'll be delving into the otherwise. But I'd love to see his show at the old Martello fort."

"Then once again, I'll be your guide." Rex stopped in front of her house, and she got out before he could open the door.

"Thanks for the tour. I appreciated it."

"I'll be looking forward to this evening. More than you know."

Chapter Nineteen

Katie unlocked her office then flung open the doors and windows. Returning to the small, bricked garden, she picked a golden alamanda blossom to brighten the dark day and floated it in a bowl on her desk before she began planning her interview with Elizabeth Wright.

When the telephone rang, she answered, then leaned forward, smiling.

"How's the case going, Katie girl?"

"Like the ebb tide. Lots of energy going out, but little coming in. Wish you were here to advise and suggest."

"Who's your prime suspect? Po?"

"Do you think he should be?"

"Not necessarily. But victim's spouses usually rate a large chunk of a detective's time."

"Are you beginning to think the police could have been wrong?"

"That's always a possibility, but no. My opinion remains unchanged."

"As yet, I've reached no conclusions. Po's alibi is like Swiss cheese, but I've crossed Diane and Randy Dade off my list. And Mary Bethel, Alexa's secretary. Likewise Beck Dixon and Rex Layton."

"The mayor's suspect?"

"No longer." She explained Rex's relationship to Alexa Chitting and the Cayo Hueso project. "I still have three people to talk to — Alexa's lover, Po's mistress, and Elizabeth Wright."

"Why Wright? Who's she?"

"Head of the Department of Community Affairs. If Alexa's second will had been valid, it could have indirectly affected Elizabeth Wright's job."

"How?"

She sighed, but maybe rehashing the material for Mac would help clarify it in her own mind. "Wright makes decisions on Key West land usage. At one time both she and the mayor favored building a low-rent housing development on old salt pond land. Then Elizabeth did a sudden about-face, deciding that the land was inappropriate and that it should be preserved."

"That makes her suspect? If the second will had been valid, the Preservation Group would probably have used Alexa's fortune to fight Cayo Hueso. If that were Wright's desire, then she certainly wouldn't have offed Alexa before she could sign that will."

"But there's more craziness. Wright did another turn-around the day after Alexa's murder and is again considering the salt pond location for development. Something there stinks, but so far I haven't learned what it is."

"Politics. There can be a lot of politics and insider dealing in any public building program. Wright's connection with the murder seems tenuous to me, but it's your case."

"You're probably right, but I'd like to know what motivated her vacillation. I smell big bucks in the Cayo Hueso machinations, and Wright's nose is sharper and more experienced than mine. She knows she must produce if she's to step up on the career ladder."

"Well, give the Chittings their money's worth, Katie girl. Hang in there. Phone me if you have any problems I can help you solve."

"Thanks. I will."

"I just called to tell you that I've had some good breaks here and I may be back by Monday night."

"Great!"

"You can tell me more about the case then, if you haven't already solved it. But take care. A person who closes in on a killer puts himself at risk. Herself, in your case."

"I'll be cautious and I'll see you on Monday."

She sat thinking, wishing she could solve the case before Mac returned. What a plum that would be! Still smiling at the thought, she tucked a notebook into her bag and left the office. The cold front had worsened and she shivered as she walked the few blocks to Elizabeth Wright's Simonton Street office.

She tried to hold her mind on questions

she would ask, but her thoughts kept flying to Rex. How deeply had he been involved with Elizabeth Wright? Diane had called him a ladies' man. Was he the kind who made a conquest then moved on? Maybe she was merely his next target. No time to speculate about that now. She had arrived.

"Katie Hassworth," she said to the secretary, a short, plump brunette who was retouching her nail polish. "I've a ten o'clock appointment."

"Yes, Miss Hassworth. Go right in. Miss Wright's expecting you."

Thank you, Miss Scarlet Nails. Sometimes she could identify with Bubba's need for nicknames. She stubbed her toe on a loosely woven rattan rug as she stepped into a pine-paneled office and she felt her face flush. Some entrance! Elizabeth Wright rose, sending a musky scent across her huge oak desk. Even in her tailored business suit she exuded that sexy glamour Beck had scorned. And if she recalled seeing Katie at Alexa's marina office, she gave no indication of it.

"Do have a chair, Miss Hassworth." She glanced at her watch. "I know you've come concerning the Chitting murder, but I can't imagine how I can help you."

Katie sat, Elizabeth Wright's cool aplomb making her feel like a recalcitrant student called to the principal's office for reprimand. Two file folders lay in precision-like order on the left side of the desk, brass bookends supported three volumes on the right side, and a single golden hibiscus blossom floated in a brandy snifter near the telephone. It hardly looked like the desk of a person who had trouble making decisions.

"I just wanted to discuss the murder in general."

"Why with me?" Elizabeth Wright met her direct gaze.

"Because of your interest in Cayo Hueso. Alexa Chitting hated to see that project located in the salt pond area."

"I understood that she had fists-up feelings about it."

"You didn't know her?"

"No. Not personally. Of course, everyone in Key West knew of her."

"I've been reading newspaper accounts and I notice that on several occasions you've changed your position on the location of the Cayo Hueso development."

Wright smiled and shrugged. "You know how reporters misquote and exaggerate."

Katie consulted her notebook. "A month before Alexa's murder — that would have been in December — you were in favor of the salt pond location for Cayo Hueso, right?"

"Yes. I thought that abandoned area could be utilized for the benefit of many people. Mayor Layton agreed, and he was ready to use his influence with the city council to help get the project underway."

"But on the Friday before Alexa Chitting died, you changed your mind about the suitability of the location. Is that correct?"

"Yes. Yes, I believe I did have some second thoughts around that time."

"Why?"

"Why?" She feigned surprise.

"Yes, why?" Katie let the silence between them burgeon until Wright responded, her speech now a bit faster and louder.

"I did some further checking. Key West is an area of critical state concern, and the DCA has the final say in local land-use issues."

Double talk. "Why did you change your mind?"

Wright cleared her throat and folded her hands on her desk blotter. "You sound as if you're about to read me my rights. Should I call my lawyer?"

"I'm not with the police department, Miss Wright. You'll be a great help to me if you'll give candid answers. Why did you change your mind about Cayo Hueso?"

"I wanted to do more checking. The density of the project nagged at me. Overcrowding would be a detriment to the community. During the peak tourist season, the island teems with visitors. As you know, this annual surge of humanity taxes our water supply and our electric generators as well as our patience."

Katie checked her notes again. "I understand that in December, the density of the projected Cayo Hueso complex had already been reduced from five hundred and fifty units to four hundred."

"You've done your homework well."

"What else caused you to change your mind?"

Elizabeth unfolded her hands, placed them in her lap, refolded them. "I reconsidered traffic patterns. Traffic's always a problem here, and I felt cars from Cayo Hueso might clog the main artery of Roosevelt Boulevard."

"Mayor Layton backed the project. What did he think about the traffic pattern?"

She raised her chin slightly. "Perhaps you should direct that question to Mayor Layton personally."

"Yes, perhaps I should. But the fact remains that shortly before Alexa Chitting's death you changed your mind, protesting the use of the salt pond area for the housing complex."

"Yes, yes I did."

"Could I see the papers involved in this project? Blueprints? Contracts? That sort of thing."

Wright hesitated, then smiled. "No. I'm afraid that's impossible."

"Why? The documents are public records, are they not?"

"Yes. They are public, but at this time they are out of my office."

"Where are they?"

She flushed. "At the state office in Tallahassee." Her voice cracked and she cleared her throat.

Katie sensed a lie, but there was no way she could circumvent Wright's refusal at this point. And she wasn't sure she would have known what to do with the papers had she won access to them, but Elizabeth Wright's reaction to her request intrigued her.

"On the day after Alexa's murder you returned to your first position, again backing the project. I'm interested in this vacillation."

"Why are you relating my decisions to the time of Alexa Chitting's murder?" Wright rose and stood behind her chair, gripping its back with her right hand. "I never thought in those terms."

"I'm investigating a grisly killing. I try to relate everything of importance that was happening at that time to the moment of Alexa's death. Will you explain why you again became enthusiastic about the salt pond locating for Cayo Hueso?"

"I don't know why you're besetting me with this line of questioning. The mayor liked the salt pond locale, and I'm afraid I let some of his enthusiasm influence me."

"You're a businesswoman in a responsible position. I find it astonishing that you'd let personal matters sway such an important decision."

"I didn't. Not really, that is. But Mayor

Layton's position made me think. I began to delve more carefully into the details involved. And I agree with him. I think land that has all the visual status of an eyesore would better serve humanity if someone developed and utilized it."

"Then why haven't you signed the necessary papers?"

"Any decision of this magnitude requires much careful thought. I plan to sign the papers, but not until the lawyers in Tallahassee have scrutinized all the fine print."

"Then you have no strong feeling about preserving the area as a historical site?"

"No. None. I see it as trashy land that can be turned into a financial and social asset to Key West."

"Where were you on the Monday night Alexa Chitting died?"

Wright snorted and sat back down at her desk. "You suspect *me* of doing her in?"

"I'm hired to suspect anyone with motive and opportunity. I merely asked where you were the night of her death."

"I never thought I'd need an alibi, but of course I have one. I was in Naples on business. I took an early morning flight on Monday and returned mid-afternoon on Tuesday. I'm sure airport records will corroborate my words."

"I'll check it out." Katie rose. "Thank you for your time, Miss Wright."

Chapter Twenty

Back in her office, Katie paced, thinking about Elizabeth Wright, her attitude toward being interrogated, her responses. Had Rex influenced her decisions as much as she claimed? Maybe she *should* ask Rex. No. Considering their current friendship, he surely might misinterpret her motives and consider such queries self serving. She made a note to check on the times of Elizabeth's departure from and return to Key West. Once she could scratch her off the suspect list, she would also write her out of her private life.

"Dear child, may I come in?" Beck Dixon paused in the office doorway as if posing for a photograph.

"Of course. Come in and sit down." Katie rose, watching the older woman smooth the front of her blue pantsuit as she sat in the straight chair across from her desk. "What brings you out on this blustery morning?"

"Extraordinary news." Beck paused, glanced at the door, and Katie closed it.

"What sort of news?"

Beck took a deep breath, exhaled, then let her gaze bore into Katie. "Angie's pregnant. By Po Chitting."

Katie sat down at her desk, unable to break away from Beck's piercing gaze. "You're sure?"

"She confided in me this morning. She found out a while back, and she was so devastated she kept the news to herself, trying to decide on a course of action. She's told nobody until today."

"She's sure Po's the father?"

"Positive. Dear child, Angie's not some blowsy tart. She's never been promiscuous. She's as dedicated to Po as if they were legally married."

"Does she want an abortion?"

"Never. She's delighted at the thought of having a child, but she finds the circumstances unthinkable. So far I'm the only one she's told. I thought you'd be interested and I know you'll be discreet."

"This makes both Angie and Po stronger suspects in the case. You realize that, don't you?"

"I disagree. Angie's hardly the type to bash someone with a conch shell just because she's pregnant."

"Are you sure? In a closely-knit Cuban family, an out-of-wedlock pregnancy would be considered a sin as well as a social disgrace and an unforgivable embarrassment. Given Angie Garcia's family background, I think her condition could motivate murder. With Alexa out of the way, Angie and Po would be free to marry. Hers would not be the first baby in the history of humankind to arrive a few weeks early."

"In your grubby business, I suppose you have to look at it that way, but I don't. Angie's a good woman who's been trapped by passion. She's not a murderer."

"You may be right, but I'll have to talk to her." Katie glanced uneasily at Beck.

"I understand. I've told her you'd want to see her, told her I was helping with the investigation. She hates the idea, of course, but I promised her you'd be kind as well as discreet, that her secret would go no further unless revealing it was essential to solving the case."

"And she agreed to talk with me?"

"Not in so many words. You'll have to set up the meeting. But at least your request won't come as a total shock."

"Thanks for telling me this. I appreciate it."

Beck stood. "You're welcome. I empathize with Angie. She deserves better than Po Chitting. She's like a good potato tossed into a bad stew."

"Po's free. Maybe they'll marry. He seems devoted to his grandchildren as well as to Angie. Perhaps he'll welcome another child."

"And with the Chitting millions, the child will lack for nothing. Is that what you're thinking?"

"Something like that."

"Could I go along when you talk with

Angie? It would help put her at ease."

"Yes. That'd be okay with me, if she agrees."

"I think she's home. Why not call her now? Thursday's her day off."

Katie dialed. Angie Garcia answered on the first ring and agreed to the meeting.

"She seemed almost eager to talk with us," Katie said as they drove the short distance to South Roosevelt Boulevard and Angie's houseboat.

"That doesn't surprise me, nor should it surprise you. I paved the way."

At the seawall, pelicans and gulls perched on gray pilings, and the chilling wind carried a fetid odor of brine weed and dead fish. Katie followed Beck to the tired-looking boat whose cabin mimicked a Swiss chalet.

"Bubba told me about this, and I doubted him." In spite of the dank cold and the smell of death, Katie managed to smile at the houseboat with its green paint peeling like sunburnt skin, its steeply pitched roof, and its pseudo-balcony. The blooming geraniums on the balcony offered the only fresh touch to the scene. "Some place."

Beck nodded. "It seems at odds with the sea as well as with its neighbors."

Katie eyed the adjacent crafts which were a weathered gray and which looked as if a large wave could send them gurgling to the silty bottom. Clearly, Angie Garcia had a mind and an imagination of her own.

As Katie stepped from the seawall onto the red carpeted gangplank leading to the houseboat's deck, Angie opened the cabin door. By habit, Katie tried to pinpoint Angie's age, but like many Cuban women, she wore agelessness like a shield and it served her well. Slim but well rounded, she held herself with the proud air of a flamenco dancer as she tightened the sash on her red silk robe, and Katie wondered if Angie knew she looked like the cliché most men associated with Cuban women.

"Buenas dias, ladies."

"Buenas dias." Katie unconsciously imitated Angie's musical Spanish as she and Beck crossed the small deck and stepped inside Angie's tiny living room where a picture of Christ and a gold-painted crucifix hung on the wall above a couch. A plaster model of the Virgin Mary stood on a coffee table, and the aroma of freshly baked bread filled the cabin.

"Please sit down." Angie scooted brown rattan chairs across the planked floor, placing them nearer the coffee table, and once Katie and Beck were seated, she sat on the couch across from them. The lulling motion of the boat lessened the jarring effect of Swiss chalet and Cuban décor.

"You've come to discuss the murder."

Katie liked Angie's directness. "Yes. I understand that you and Po Chitting are . . . companions."

"Yes. We are long-time friends and lovers. But I did not murder Alexa Chitting."

"Katie is making no accusations, Angie." Beck leaned forward, smiling, but Angie ignored her.

"Had murder been my goal, it would not have taken me so many years to bring it about." Her nostrils flared and her dark eyes narrowed to slits.

"Did you hate Alexa Chitting?"

"No."

"What was your relationship to her?"

"Relationship? Hah! We had no relationship."

"How did you feel toward her?"

"I felt sorry for her."

"Sorry? Why?"

"Because I possessed the love of her gentle, kind man and she had nada. Zip. I don't believe Po Chitting is capable of hate, but if he had been, he would have hated Alexa."

"I see."

"No, I don't think you see at all." Angie leaned forward, her eyes flashing, her hoop earrings swaying, the three gold bangles on her right arm jangling.

"Angie! Angie!" Beck rose and sat beside Angie on the couch, patting her hand. "Katie's trying to help you. Calm down."

"It is no time for calmness. People say my

Po's a sinner because he spend many sweet nights here with me. Peasants! Sometimes infidelity to the marriage vows is more self-preservation than sin. Alexa is the murderer. Alexa killed his spirit. I revived it."

"Miss Garcia, where were you on the night Alexa Chitting was murdered?"

"You do suspect me, then?"

"I merely ask a routine question. Where were you?"

"That is most easy to answer. On Monday nights I work as a cocktail waitress at Rico's on Stock Island. That is where I spent Monday night a week ago."

"And you have people who will vouch for this?"

"Rico himself. Mondays are slow. I am his only waitress on that night. If I had left, he would have missed me. It never happened. Ask Rico. Ask his customers. For you I will get names. A petition I will circulate."

"That'll be unnecessary, Miss Garcia. I'll check with Rico, of course. Today, if possible. Did you see Po on that Monday night?"

"I did not."

"He didn't come here to this house on that Monday?"

Angie hesitated, then her shoulders slumped. "Yes. Po came here that night, but for a few moments only. And I did not see him. You see, he hates my working at Rico's. He feels it's degrading, but I say that no honest work is degrading. Nevertheless, on Monday nights Po comes here and leaves a rosebud at my door to remind me that we might have spent the evening together. He has the heart and soul of a true romantic."

So Bubba had been right. He had seen Po here the Monday night of the murder. And Jib Persky? Did he know of Po's Monday night habit? Had he been trying to protect Po by saying he hadn't noticed him leave the bar that night? Po had left Captain Tony's and returned unnoticed. Perhaps he'd had another mission, other than leaving a rosebud at Angie's door.

"But you insist on this Monday job?" Katie asked.

"Yes. I need the money. I am an independent person and I pay my own bills."

Katie understood Beck's admiration for Angie, but she continued her questions. "Tell me, has Alexa Chitting's death changed your plans?"

"What plans?"

"Any plans. Perhaps plans concerning Po Chitting."

Angie turned to look at Beck. "You have told this inquisitive one of my . . . my pregnancy, yes?"

"Yes, she has." Katie answered for Beck. "But the information will go no farther. Do you and Po plan to marry?"

"Po does not know of my condition."

220

"Why have you kept it from him?"

"Still I am deciding what to do. I am in a bad situation. I have brought disgrace to myself and my family, but I want Po to feel no obligation to marry me."

"Po loves you, Angie," Beck said. "I doubt that he would consider marriage an obligation."

"Who can say!" Angie twisted her scarlet sash.

"Alexa Chitting's death puts Po in a position to marry you," Katie pointed out.

"Miss Hassworth, are you suggesting that in this way I have intentionally . . ."

"I'm suggesting nothing. I'm investigating a murder and both you and Po had strong motivations to remove Alexa from the scene."

"But we did not. We were both happy with the arrangement of our lives."

"But the fact remains that now you both might become even happier."

"You will please to leave my house." Angie stood and pointed to the door. "Not you, Beck. You stay, but the detective, go. Out! Out!" When Katie was slow to rise, Angie picked up the statue of the Virgin, brandishing it in her right hand.

"Thank you for talking with me, Miss Garcia." Katie rose and ran, jogging down the gangplank and to her car, wondering if Angie could have wielded the conch shell. Had her hot temper flared in a confrontation with Alexa?

In a few moments, Beck joined Katie.

"Some lady," Katie said. "Some temper."

"I apologize for her outburst. It's her condition. Try to understand."

"I do understand."

"You will check on her alibi?"

"Yes, of course. You may see Angie as a good girl gone astray, and you may be right. But she could also be an angry conniving woman after a share of the Chitting millions which she thinks should rightfully be hers."

"I don't believe that. Not for one minute. Po would have supported her, had she expected that of a lover. She could have been sharing the Chitting fortune for years, but no. She chose to be her own person."

"Angie may work hard for a living, for her independence, but that certainly doesn't mean she'd be willing to support Po Chitting. That might have been in the offing, had Alexa's new will been legalized, had Angie and Po's relationship continued. Po would have found himself very short of rosebud funds."

Katie drove Beck to her car at the agency, then she headed across the Boca Chica Bridge to Stock Island. Rico's Bar and Grill. She had driven only a short distance before she saw it on her right. She pulled to the front entrance and stopped, sitting for a few moments to organize her thoughts before she confronted Angie's employer.

Chapter Twenty-One

A red and white closed sign hung on the weathered pine door of Rico's Bar, but when Katie pounded on the entry, she heard shuffling footsteps inside. She hunched her shoulders as the dank wind knifed her back.

"Hold your horses. I'm coming."

When the door opened, she looked up at a gangling old man wearing a blue muscle shirt, chino cutoffs, and thongs. If he was aware of the fact that his body looked cadaverous, he didn't let on. A plastic scrub brush floated in the bucket of gray-black water he carried in one gnarled hand and he ran his other hand over his balding head as he squinted at her from piercing blue eyes. He shook his head.

"We ain't open, miss. Too early. Come back around five this afternoon."

"I need to talk to Rico. Will he be here then?"

"I'm Rico. Rico Lopez. If I owe you money, don't come back at five. Wait 'til the first of the month. Go now. You're letting in cold air."

She squelched a smile, wondering how many bill collectors were able to penetrate

Rico's air of imperturbability. She showed the man her identification. "I'm investigating the Chitting murder, Mr. Lopez." She saw his eyes widen for a moment, then his face closed, mask-like.

"Don't know nothing about no murder. And don't want to know nothing about no murder." He started to close the door, but Katie took a peremptory step forward.

"Wait. Let me ask just two questions. Do you remember the night of the murder? It happened a week ago last Monday — be two weeks this coming Monday."

"I remember. Got a friend who knows . . . the Chittings."

"Did Angie Garcia work here on the Monday night Alexa Chitting was murdered?"

"Yes. She works here every Monday."

"She was here all night?"

"That's three questions. You said two."

"Was she here all night?"

Rico started to close the door. "Yes. Angie came in a little before five and she didn't leave until midnight."

"She took no breaks?"

"She took twenty minutes to eat her supper. Then she took a fifteen-minute break around nine o'clock for a cup of coffee. But she never left the place."

"You're sure?"

"She's my only waitress on Mondays and

she was here all night." Rico ran his hand over his chin. "Guess Pete Harris could vouch for Angie, too, if my word ain't enough for you. He's here when I open. He's here when I close. Some day I'm going to start charging the bastard rent."

"Thank you, Mr. Lopez. You've been a help."

"Yeah, sure."

He closed the door and she heard the lock snap in place as she turned to leave. Another name off her list. She was glad Angie's alibi held up. The woman had enough problems.

For lunch, Katie ate grapes and a peach at her desk as she mulled over the remaining suspects, their possible motivations for murdering Alexa Chitting, their alibis. At the end of the afternoon she felt no closer to pinpointing the culprit than she had the day she accepted the case, and she mentioned that to Rex when he called for her for dinner.

"Maybe tonight will open some new avenues for your investigation." Rex stood on the veranda for a moment, slapping his car keys against his palm as if deep in thought, then he took her arm and they walked to his Corvette.

"Why don't we drive to East Martello and see the Parish show right now? We'll beat some of the crowd and we can have a more relaxed dinner later."

"Good idea." Katie settled herself more comfortably, turning slightly so she could see Rex easily. "Look at us, Rex. White slacks. Red shirts. White sandals. We look like a matched set."

"You make us sound like golf clubs." He smiled down at her. "But I knew from the moment I first saw you that we had lots in common."

"What's Tyler Parish like?" She leaned a bit toward him as he covered her hand with his.

"I don't know him well, but he has a reputation around town as a ladies' man."

"The two of you must have a lot in common then?" She grinned at him. "Your way with the ladies is one of the first thing I heard about you, too."

"Untrue. Never listen to gossip. Now . . . you were asking about Parish. I consider him a serious artist in spite of his playboy ways and his Don Juan image. He turns out lots of work and it's beginning to catch on with the critics as well as with the public."

"He's evidently not self-supporting."

"Who knows? He could afford to be casual about money matters. Why should he worry about supporting himself when he had Alexa?"

"Right. Why?"

Rex pulled into a parking lot. "Here we are. You can meet him and make your own judgments."

As he helped her from the car, she paused, shivering a bit as she watched early-evening shadows play against the blood-red brick of the Martello Tower. "I suppose you know all about this place, its history, I mean."

"Are you humoring me? You know, the old 'be interested in what he's interested in' routine?"

"Of course not." She laughed. "I'm sincerely interested in this place — only to a mild degree, of course."

"I know some of its history, and I'll stop at your first yawn. Both the East and West Martello Towers were built during the Civil War, and the men stationed here were supposed to assist the troops at Fort Taylor in repelling any coastal landing forces."

"But enemy forces never arrived, right?"

"You've been reading up on the place."

"A good detective has to be prepared. I did do some reading."

"So you probably already know that neither tower was completed, and that cannons were never installed. Before the Art and Historical Society took over this tower about forty years ago, it had no roof. Now the roof's complete and visitors can climb to the top for an overview of this island city and the surrounding area."

"I'd like to do that sometime." She linked her arm through his as they approached the arched entryway and stepped inside the old fortification. The musty smell of damp masonry filled her nostrils and she wondered how paintings survived the dank atmosphere.

"The gallery has rotating shows of contemporary and local art," Rex said. "Artists consider it an honor to have their work hanging on these walls. The gallery also houses permanent collections of Stanley Papio weldings and Mario Sanchez wood carvings."

As Rex guided her into a room on their left, she tightened her grip on his arm. "Look."

Po Chitting and Mary Bethel stood in one corner with their backs to them. When they heard footsteps grate against cement, they turned.

"Good evening," Po said. "A nice exhibit." He nodded toward the paintings. Mary Bethel stood at his side, silently looking up at him.

"Parish is making a name for himself in the area," Rex said, picking up two catalogs from a table that also held a guest register. "I've been looking forward to seeing a collection of his works."

"Do either of you paint?" Katie asked, wishing they could gracefully break away from these two.

"No," Mary said. "We write, don't we, Po?"

Po smiled. "Yes. We write."

Katie turned to sign the guest register,

wondering if Mary knew about Po and his relationship. Could she see herself taking Alexa's place in Po's life?

"Nice seeing you," Rex said to Po and Mary as he ended the awkward encounter by guiding Katie toward painting number one. "We're going to view the collection in order."

Katie waited until Po and Mary were out of earshot before she spoke. "Why do you suppose they're here together?"

"No reason they shouldn't be. They're both into the arts. Maybe Po feels an obligation to Mary. She's doing him a favor by keeping Alexa's office open."

"That's true." Katie thought about Angie and wondered what she'd think of Po and Mary as a twosome. And why would Po be interested in Parish's work? On the other hand, why wouldn't he be interested? It was something to consider — tomorrow.

She guessed that there were easily over fifty seascapes and sea-oriented paintings lining the walls of the room. All of the works were for sale and the price tags were impressive. Some paintings were framed and some were not, but Katie felt their mesmerizing effect. Tyler Parish knew the sea and knew it well; the power of his work permeated the room. When they had almost finished viewing the exhibit, she was studying the blended colors in a sunset scene when Rex touched her arm.

"Katie, I'd like you to meet Tyler Parish."

She turned, ready to smile, but upon seeing the artist her whole body tensed. This was the man in the VW who repeatedly had driven past her office. This was the man she had seen leaving the artists' loft as she entered. Why had he been spying on her! A wariness filled her as her mental picture of Tyler Parish shattered and she pigeonholed the dreamy, otherworld quality she usually associated with artists. This man looked like the kind who ate rare steak for breakfast. Fortyish. Medium height. Beefy shoulders and thighs matched square, ham-like hands. The smell of oil paints and turpentine clung to his faded jeans and muslin poncho. She imagined that the smell also clung to his scraggly red hair and full beard.

"Mr. Parish." Katie offered her hand and he shook it in a bone-crushing grip. "I'm pleased to meet you at last and I'm enjoying viewing your paintings." Was that the right thing to say? Suddenly she felt inept as well as frightened.

Parish jammed his hands into his pockets and looked at her from eyes the color of hemp rope. This crude-looking man had bedded the elegant Alexa? She tried to squelch her imagination as well as her wariness.

"You're the private investigator in the Chitting murder?" Parish asked. "We've talked on the phone?"

"Yes." Katie hid her surprise at his questions.

Surely he was well aware of her identity, well aware of their recent conversation.

Parish chuckled. "You don't meet my mental stereotype of a female detective."

"Sorry to disappoint, but rest assured that I won't trouble you with questions tonight."

"No trouble. I apologize for my brusqueness when we talked earlier. My mind was on preparations for this show. Fact is, now that the show's underway, I'd like to get your questions behind me."

"Well . . ."

"There's a quiet room across the corridor. Why don't we go there and talk? Will you excuse us, Mayor?"

"If it suits Katie to talk with you now, of course I'll excuse you." Rex looked at her for confirmation.

She felt thrown off balance. She preferred setting up her own interviews and she resented Tyler Parish taking such strong initiative. She also felt it imperative that he not be cognizant of her insecurity.

"If Rex will excuse us, I'd appreciate the chance to talk with you, Mr. Parish, and I'll be brief."

Rex nodded his consent, and Tyler Parish led the way to an unoccupied room where the Sanchez works were on exhibit. There were no chairs, so they stood near the doorway.

"Fire away, Katie Hassworth, P.I." Parish

leaned against a wall, his gaze boring into hers.

"Since brashness seems to be the order of the day, perhaps I should begin by asking if you murdered Alexa Chitting."

He laughed. "I like your style. I like women who say what's on their minds. But no. I didn't murder Alexa. Why would one do away with the goose that was laying the golden eggs? It would make no sense."

"I understand your work's catching on — that you've been invited to hang one-man shows in important places. Perhaps your life-style, your occupation no longer needed Alexa Chitting's financial support."

"My occupation? Painting isn't my occupation. It's my *life*. Let's get this straight. Alexa Chitting supported me through the hard years when I might have died, and I'll be ever grateful to her for that."

"So grateful that you're frequently observed in other cities with other women?"

"I see you have a sharp eye for detail."

"Why were you scrutinizing my office?"

"I'd heard you were investigating for the Chittings. I wanted to see the person who might possibly deal me a lot of grief."

"You weren't very subtle."

"Subtle's never been my style."

"Why did you avoid me at your art studio?"

Parish looked blank. "I've never seen you at the studio."

She let it pass. Maybe he'd been so engrossed in this show that he hadn't noticed her — or hadn't recognized her. "Where were you on Monday night a week ago?"

He met her direct gaze. "I felt ill that evening and I stayed at home resting and reading."

This man ill? She could hardly imagine it. It was equally difficult to imagine him spending a quiet evening with a book. "Were you with anyone who might vouch for your presence that night?"

"Sorry to disappoint you, but I was alone. I can't prove it, of course. But neither can you disprove it. It's one of those alibis you detectives hate, isn't it?"

"No, Mr. Parish. It's really no alibi at all. When did you last see Alexa alive?"

"That fateful Monday around noon. She stopped by my place for . . . a chat. I never saw her again. Of course, that's another statement I can't prove." He smiled. "Nor can you refute it."

Determined to take charge of the situation, she looked directly at him. "Who do you think might have hated Mrs. Chitting enough to kill her?"

"People don't become as wealthy as Alexa was without making some enemies along the way, but I know of nobody who wanted to see her dead."

"Thank you for your time, Mr. Parish. That will be all the questions for now." She turned, left the room, and rejoined Rex in the other gallery. "Ready to go?"

"You're finished viewing the show?"

"Yes. Let's go, please."

They left East Martello, and Rex drove toward Old Town. "Did you learn anything important from Parish?"

"On the night of the murder he was home alone."

"Not much help."

"None. I try to keep an open mind, but I dislike that man."

"Any special reason?"

"He's overbearing. Blatant. Posturing." She wanted to call him a sneak, but in all fairness she couldn't. A sneak wouldn't have circled her block five times in broad daylight and while driving a bright yellow car. "I had the feeling that behind all his hubris he was secretly laughing at me. He took delight in presenting an alibi that could be neither proved nor disproved."

"Then I'm sorry I placed you in the position of having to talk business with him without the proper preparation."

"I doubt there could have been any proper preparation for a meeting with Tyler Parish. I can't imagine him and Alexa Chitting . . ."

Rex laughed. "Let's forget about Parish for tonight."

"That's fine with me."

"I've a surprise for you. I've bought steaks

and some Idaho bakers, and I'll treat you to a home-cooked dinner at my place if you'll toss a salad."

A night for surprises, she thought, again feeling off balance. She was not at all sure she wanted to share an intimate dinner at Rex's home, and not at all sure she wanted to offend him by refusing.

Chapter Twenty-Two

"How can I turn down an offer like that! You're playing to my major weakness. Food."

"Good. All detectives should have at least one major weakness."

He drove to Caroline Street and parked in front of a two-story house surrounded by a white privacy fence.

"So this is what you bought instead of a hotel?"

"Right. Like it?"

"It's unusual. And yes, I like it. Since it appealed to you, I assume it's steeped in island history."

"Right again. Local carpenters built the house before the Civil War and it's called an eyebrow house. The style's unique to Key West."

She admired the home with its peaked roof and slender porch posts which rose from the porch floor to the second story eave. "Why the name eyebrow?"

"See the series of small windows set close beneath the roof overhang? If you use your imagination they can remind one of eyebrows — hence the name. And that's all the history lesson for tonight — at least until we make history of those steaks I've had marinating since morning."

She followed him inside the high-ceilinged house, through a deeply carpeted central hallway and into a kitchen ruled by stainless steel and white porcelain. Its sliding glass doors opened onto a tropical garden and pool where philodendron and bougainvillea twined between sea grape trees. As Rex stepped onto the patio to light pool-side torches and the grill, the fragrance of jasmine wafted to them, and she saw an inflated likeness of a huge hibiscus blossom floating in azure water.

"Lovely," she murmured. "Whimsical."

Stepping back into the kitchen, Rex removed two steaks from the refrigerator. "Lovely jasmine. Lovely steaks. Only the plastic hibiscus is whimsical. But first things first. You'll find lettuce, tomatoes, avocados in the hydrator. I'll have the steaks ready by the time you've tossed the salad."

He laid the steaks on the grill, then splashed white wine into the frosted goblets he'd had chilling in the freezer. They sipped as she worked on the salad. When the meal was ready, they ate at a pool-side table in the flickering torchlight. Although the privacy fence protected them from some of the chilly wind, she allowed him to drape a white cardigan around her shoulders.

"Such a lovely setting. You must really enjoy all this."

"I do. I'd hate to have to give it up. The house has a mind of its own and so does this island."

"Key West's a city a person either loves or hates."

He cut another bite of steak. "I know what you mean. It's seedy at the same time it's eclectic."

"Right. Sometimes I feel as if someone's tried to thumbtack culture on it the same way I thumbtacked literary quotations on my classroom bulletin board."

"It's fanciful and freewheeling. It's also dignified, stylish, and grand." He winked. "It's my kind of city."

"And mine. I think the thing I like most is its excess of individuality. I like its live-and-let-live attitude."

He peered at her over the rim of his wineglass. "Katie, tell me more about yourself. I want to know you better."

"There's nothing more to tell."

"There's always more to tell. Your ambitions. Your goals. What do you expect to be doing five years from now? Do you intend to spend the rest of your life solving murder cases?"

"Do you intend to spend the rest of your life being mayor of Key West?"

"I think I'd like that, if it were possible. But we were talking about you. Do you really like being a private detective? How does it compare to teaching English?"

"Are you subtly insinuating that I should return to the classroom?"

"No way. I'm just trying to learn how you feel about your life — past, present, and future."

She leaned back, enjoying the relaxing effect of the wine, the cool night. "I want my life to count for something. I almost lost it in the classroom, but now I feel as if I've been granted a second chance."

"Everyone's life counts for something. Who's to say it's more important to try to teach the sonnet form to kids who prefer to glamorize the lyrics of Michael Jackson than it is to take criminals off the streets?"

"Or to plan additional housing developments for an island city that's already overcrowded? Everyone has to do his own thing, I suppose. But I'm a coward."

"I doubt that."

"I still have nightmares about Jon McCartel and I can't face returning to the classroom. Can you imagine what it's like to have a child shoot you?"

"Is it worse than risking a pot shot from some known or unknown criminal? You're risking your life every day in your job."

"To see a child wield a gun vitiates the spirit."

"Do you carry a gun in your work?"

"Sometimes. Sometimes not. I like the

'sometimes not' the best."

"Have you put any criminals behind bars?"

"A few. Druggies. But I've dealt mostly with cases involving missing persons. Not too much danger there."

"When you send some creeps to jail, how long do you think they'll be off the streets? If they hold grudges, who do you think they'll look up first when they're released? I hate seeing you in such dangerous work. Have you thought of its long-term ramifications?"

"Nobody's taken a shot at Katie Hassworth, P.I. That's more than I can say about Katie Hassworth, middle school English teacher."

"But someone might. I worry about you."

"Don't worry. I can take care of myself."

"If you get too close to the person who killed Alexa Chitting, you'll *really* be jeopardizing your life. A person who could bash in a head with a conch shell wouldn't hesitate to kill you if you threatened to expose him. Think about that."

"Him? You think a man killed Alexa?"

"Probably. But that's not my point. My point is that you're in constant danger."

"But I'm on guard. In that classroom, I was totally vulnerable. Who would have thought . . . but enough about me. Enough. You've told me about your stint in Africa and your coming to the Keys, but I sense that you're holding something back." She grinned at him. "What about the women in your life? Have you been married?"

"No. There are no ex-wives cluttering my past."

"Strange. I can imagine that lots of women would have liked to be Mrs. Rex Layton. How have you avoided them all?"

"It wasn't all that hard, and I learned early on to avoid situations that threaten to en-snare."

"You consider marriage a snare?"

"Don't you?"

"Frankly, yes. Who needs it? I like thinking for myself. I like earning my own money — and spending it according to my own whims. I like coming and going as I please — no questions asked or answered."

"My thoughts exactly."

"But you have that ladies' man reputation."

"It figures, doesn't it? Think about it. If I surround myself with lots of women friends, no one of them can endanger my freedom."

"I'll bet lots of them have tried."

"Flattery. Flattery." He pushed his chair back from the table then helped her to her feet. "Care for a moonlight swim?"

She shivered and pulled the cardigan more closely around her shoulders. "It's too cold tonight."

"The pool's heated. I swim under the stars all winter. Come on."

She stooped at pool side and waggled her

fingers in the water. "It's lovely, but I didn't bring my suit."

"Sure you need one?"

"Absolutely sure."

"In that case, I have a few on hand for just such occasions." He led her to the guest bedroom. "Bottom drawer to the right. Take your choice." He left, closing the door behind him.

Katie opened the bottom drawer and held up three suits. Green. Yellow. Red. Bikini. Tank style. French cut. Which one had Elizabeth Wright worn? Or perhaps Elizabeth was the type who felt no necessity to wear any of them. Katie slipped into the yellow tank model. When she walked to pool side, Rex was doing laps in the deep end. She dived in, joining him, relaxing at the touch of the warm water.

"Do you suppose the neighbors are watching our craziness?" She glanced at the windows of the nearby houses.

"No, I'm sure they aren't. The privacy fence blocks the view from ground floor windows, and before I rented those two houses, I hung their second story shutters with the louvers upside down. We're alone."

They swam the length of the pool, then Rex hauled himself onto the floating hibiscus and pulled her up, molding his body to hers as the chilly air raised goosebumps on their flesh. They lay warmed by a close embrace until she forgot about conch shells and murders and artist suspects who looked like stevedores. Rex kissed the back of her neck and ran his warm hands along her arms and thighs until she turned to face him and let her lips yield to his.

When they accidentally slipped from the hibiscus float into the satiny water, Rex held her to him, kissing her again and again and again. Her strong response left her gasping for breath. No longer trusting her emotions, she forced herself to ease from his embrace. Swimming to the ladder, she climbed from the pool and wrapped herself in a bath sheet before she stepped inside the house.

He followed. "I've frightened you. Forgive me."

His apology astonished her. "You didn't frighten me. I frightened myself." She paused at the bedroom door, waiting for him to move back so she could close it.

"You needn't go, Katie." He took her in his arms, kissing her again until she felt her body melt against his. The temptation to stay all but overwhelmed her, but she managed to step back and smile as she closed the bedroom door. Her hands trembled as she dressed.

Later that night in her own bed, she wondered why she had come home. She had wanted Rex. He had wanted her. Yet here she was. Alone. She rose and poured herself a drink of the French Colombard she saved for guests and she sipped it on the cold porch balcony overlooking Old Town until she convinced herself she had done the right thing. She was not ready to be involved in a new relationship.

Dawn grayed the sky before she returned to bed and fell into a troubled sleep.

Chapter Twenty-Three

She didn't know how many times the phone had rung before she reached to answer it, sleep clogging both her mind and her voice, but as she squinted at her bedside clock, she saw it was past eight. A rage of wind carried the cries of screaming gulls, and she knew the much-touted cold front still held the island and its inhabitants in its grip.

"Good morning." Rex's voice flowed low and soft across the wire. "I've missed you. Do you realize it's been seven hours and thirty-six minutes since I've seen you?"

"You've been counting?"

"Every minute. I slept very poorly."

"So did I." Her voice caught in her throat. "You were in my thoughts, shredding any hope of sleep — until early morning. Now I've overslept."

"And it's all my fault?"

"I would be unfair to say that."

"A guy who has been rejected would like to hear that. It would be a deft and healing stroke to his ego."

"Then believe it." She threw the blanket back and sat on the edge of the bed, easing her feet into slippers and tucking her hair behind her ears.

"I'll believe it if you'll go out with me tonight. May I stop for you after work? I have a surprise in mind."

"What sort of a surprise?"

"If I told you, it would spoil it. Trust me."

"I do."

"Then I'll be at your office a little after five."

"I'll be ready. It's so good to hear from you."

"See you, Katie."

She held the phone for a few moments after their conversation ended, then she considered what she should wear that would see her through the mundane chores of the day yet look festive enough to please her on her five o'clock date. It had been good to hear from Rex — so good it made her wary of their meeting.

Please yourself, or you'll please nobody.

She showered, added a cardigan to her usual khaki skirt and shirt, then ate breakfast, resisting a second piece of toast, a second cup of coffee.

Once at her office, she picked a fresh hibiscus blossom for her desk, but she didn't open all the windows and doors. Too cold. She forgot the stale smoke smell as she consulted the phone book, then dialed an unfamiliar number. She counted eight rings.

"Air Sunshine. May I help you?"

"Katie Hassworth calling. May I speak to Mel Loring, please?"

"One moment. I'll see if he's here."

She listened to the line hum, hoping Mr. Loring worked a morning shift.

"Mel speaking."

"This is Katie Hassworth, Mr. Loring. I'm Mac McCartel's associate and I'm calling to ask a favor."

"Shoot. I owe Mac a couple."

"I need to know if Elizabeth Wright boarded an early morning flight to Naples a week ago last Monday — that would be January seven, returning on Tuesday afternoon January eight."

"One minute, please. I'll have to do some checking. That's Elizabeth Wright of Community Affairs notoriety."

"The same."

"Want to hold, or want me to return your call?"

"Will holding tie up your line too long?"

"No problem."

"Then I'll hold, thanks." The line hummed for over three minutes before Mel returned.

"Still there?"

"Of course. I appreciate your taking the time to check on this for me. Any luck?"

"Yes. Miss Wright left Key West International on the early morning flight, January seven. Seven o'clock. She returned on a mid-afternoon flight the following day, arriving at three-thirty-five on January eight. Does that help?"

"Yes. Thank you."

"You and Mac investigating the Cayo Hueso project?"

"I'm sorry, but I'm not free to say right now."

"Well, if you're taking votes, mark me against it. The island's about to sink under the weight of tourists as it is. We need more people down here like the sea needs more sharks."

"I'll keep that in mind. And I'll tell Mac you helped me out. I appreciate it."

Now what? She had hoped to find a hole in Elizabeth Wright's alibi. Wishful thinking. She started to cross Wright's name off the list, then stopped. She couldn't have been in two places at the same time, yet something about her pat alibi rang false. Katie closed her eyes, recalling the woman's cavalier manner, her smirky tone as she reeled off her alibi. Had she memorized it for the occasion?

She called information, jotted down a number in Tallahassee, then dialed.

"State Department of Community Affairs, Miss Hall speaking."

Katie identified herself. "I need to see the blueprints and any contracts or records concerning the Cayo Hueso housing project here in Key West. Those are public records, are they not?"

"Yes, Ma'am. They are. I have copies of the papers here in this office, but the original documents are in the Key West office. Miss Elizabeth Wright is in charge there. If you contact her, I'm sure she'll be glad to provide the information you need."

"Thank you." Katie replaced the receiver and stared at the telephone, thinking. So Wright had lied about the whereabouts of the papers. Reason enough to keep her name on the suspect list. Why was she keeping public documents from the public? Katie grabbed her shoulder bag and set out on foot for the Office of Community Affairs.

"Do you have an appointment with Miss Wright?" the secretary asked.

"No, I haven't. But I need to speak briefly with her."

"One moment, please. You're Miss Hassworth, right?"

Katie nodded.

The secretary thumbed a button on the intercom. "Miss Hassworth to see you." The secretary listened a moment, then turned to Katie. "Would you please state the nature of your business?"

"I've come to see the Cayo Hueso documents."

Suddenly the door to the inner office opened and Elizabeth Wright stood framed in the doorway. "Miss Hassworth, I've told you that the project documents are not here at this time. If it's important that you see them, you'll be welcome at the Tallahassee office."

"I've just telephoned that office, and Miss Hall informed me that copies of those papers are available at both offices. I would like to see your copy, please. It would save me the trip to Tallahassee."

Elizabeth Wright inhaled deeply as her face flushed and her eyes narrowed. "Will you please get the documents for Miss Hassworth, Claire?"

The secretary rose and approached the steel files behind her desk. After several moments of searching, she looked up. "The file is gone, Miss Wright. I'm sorry. I can't imagine what has . . ."

"That's all right, Claire." Elizabeth looked at Katie. "Now do you believe me? The documents are not here. If you'll excuse me now, I have work to do."

Katie left, wondering why Elizabeth Wright was lying. Or was the state department lying? Or perhaps the file was in Rex's office. Maybe some city council members had checked it out for perusal. When she returned to her office, she dialed Rex.

"Sorry, Katie. The papers aren't here and I have no idea why Elizabeth would object to your studying them."

"Thanks. See you later."

So much for that flawed theory. After lunch she spent the afternoon reviewing and typing the notes she had taken concerning the Chitting case. Sometimes reworking old material gave her new insights. But that didn't happen today. She felt her brain threatening to congeal into apathy by the time Rex arrived.

"Hard day?"

"Not too bad. My conscious mind has decided to put the case on hold and let my subconscious work on it overnight."

"Good idea. I hate sharing you with a murderer."

"What's our mysterious destination?" She settled into the Corvette as they headed north.

"We're driving to Big Pine Key to see the miniature Key deer. I'll bet you've lived in the area for two years without eyeballing those creatures."

"You're right. I have." She squelched a sigh. She didn't know what she had expected, but certainly not a wildlife tour. "What's so special about these critters?"

"Their size. Some of them are no bigger than a large dog and they're an endangered species. If we arrive around dusk, we may see a few feeding along the roadside."

"Have we brought anything for them?"

"Lots of people do bring tidbits, but that's taboo. When motorists feed them, it tends to coax them to the highway. Many are killed by vehicles every year."

"And nobody's doing anything about it?"

"Conservationists are trying. They've set

aside land as a Key deer refuge. They've placed a thirty-mile-an-hour speed limit on the road cutting through the refuge."

"And it hasn't helped?"

"Who can say for sure? They've also posted a sign near the Winn Dixie tallying the number of deer killed. Motorists can hardly help noticing it, but there's still a lot of speeding on that road."

"That's sad."

"That sign tends to be misleading, though," Rex said.

"In what way?"

"It leads people to think that people today are killing off deer that have run in the wild for ages and that's not true. When explorers first discovered these deer, there were only a few dozen of them present."

"So it's due to humans that they have increased in number, right?"

"Right. It is, and it's something to think about. I drive up to see the deer every now and then and I thought you might enjoy them, too."

"I'm glad you thought of it." She grinned at him. "The facets of your personality seem endless. Bat towers. Abandoned piers. Key deer. Salt ponds. Abused trees."

"You're poking fun."

"No. Not at all." Again she puzzled over Rex as they drove along in bumper-to-bumper traffic. Last night she had seen the hedonist who liked people, but who thought nothing of denying two families yard space so he could have a larger tropical garden and a pool. Now she was seeing a man who'd drive miles for a "maybe" chance to see some wild deer.

Once they crossed the bridge to Big Pine Key, Rex slowed the car, turning left when they reached Key Deer Boulevard. They had just passed the Winn Dixie supermarket on their right and several churches on their left, when he pulled the car to the shoulder.

"There. See him? Behind that palm on your right."

Katie peered in the direction Rex was pointing until she saw the tiny deer whose coat blended with the brown ground cover and tree trunks until it was almost invisible.

Its head was down as it grazed, then suddenly it froze, stared directly at them and bounded away, its white tail like a retreating flag.

She leaned back into the car seat. "They'd make cute pets, wouldn't they? I've seen bigger dogs."

"Look to your far right. I see another one half hidden behind that Sabal palm."

Leaning forward, she looked, but only in time to see the creature bound into the thicket. Rex drove slowly along the road, but they saw no more deer. On their return to the highway, they stopped at an abandoned gravel pit the conservationists had named the Blue Hole, but even the resident alligators were hiding from the chill air.

"Hungry?" he asked.

"Yes. Tonight could be my turn to cook. I have some grouper fillets in my freezer. We could thaw them quickly in the microwave."

"I'll take a rain check on the grouper. There's an open-air café near here. Very rustic, but the lobster's great."

"Open air? We'll freeze."

"Not so. Trust me."

"Okay."

On Ramrod Key Rex parked at Boondocks and they crossed a roofed porch to sit at a pine table that tilted when touched until Rex folded a napkin and slipped it under one leg. Roll-down plastic sheets blocked the north wind, but the waitresses wore sweaters as they took orders and served steaming cups of coffee. In spite of the cold front, tourists and locals crowded the place.

"I think the locals have a secret affection for bad weather," Rex said. "In small doses, of course."

"Maybe it's fun to talk about later — how rotten it was, and all. We used to do that a lot in Iowa after a big snow."

"Yeah, we did that in New York, too, lying about whose car was stuck the longest and who had the deepest drifts in his driveway. Seems like a long time ago."

As the place grew more crowded, they shared their table with a couple from Illinois who regaled them with information about that state's drought and poor corn crop. Rex shared facts concerning fishing bans on king mackerel. Katie tried to look interested, but she wished she and Rex were alone. Corn crops. Weather. Fish. Those were topics discussed by people who really had no common interests. The small talk made the lack of interests more palatable. She ate lobster and coleslaw until she was sure she had gained at least five pounds, then after the meal, she relaxed as they drove back to Key West and stopped in front of Rex's house.

"Forget where I live?" she asked.

"Thought we'd stop for a drink. I have some delicious after-dinner liqueur."

"Sounds good." She followed Rex inside, sitting in the warmth of the kitchen as wind howled across the patio. He poured their drinks then turned the hi-fi to soft music and joined her at the snack bar.

"It's lovely here, Rex. I feel sorry for anyone who lives north of the Boca Chica Bridge."

"Agreed." He rose and shoved a small dining table to one side. "Care to dance?"

She slipped into his arms easily and willingly, and unmindful of stove and sink, they danced slowly to golden oldies — "Stardust," "Begin the Beguine," "Night and Day" — as if they were discovering the magic of music for the first time.

"Stay here tonight," Rex said when the music died. He molded his hands around her hips, holding her to him as he blew his warm breath into her ear. "Don't leave me, Katie."

He took her hand and she followed him upstairs to the bedroom where they discovered a different kind of magic. And she stayed the night because he wanted her to and because she wanted to.

Chapter Twenty-Four

At first, when she began to waken on Saturday morning, she lay with her eyes closed, snuggling more comfortably into the warm curve of Rex's body, feeling his moist breath against her neck, breathing in the male scent of him. She smiled, remembering their lovemaking that had lasted into the early morning hours. That was how sleeping with a man should be. Rex had given her a sense of rightness — of wholeness and belonging — so different from the feeling of fragmentation and inadequacy she had felt with Chuck.

"Awake?" he murmured into her ear and brushed her cheek with a kiss.

"Almost. I'll open my eyes if you'll promise not to disappear."

"Promise."

She opened her eyes, seeing the morning's dull gray light illumine a jute-covered wall, a brown leather chair, the polished floor. Her big toe touched the smooth mahogany of the four-poster bed. A man's room.

"Glad you stayed?" He raked his fingers through his hair in the familiar gesture she knew so well.

"Very glad." Reluctantly, she sat up,

swinging her legs over the side of the bed. She groped for her shoes, her clothes.

"For one who's so very glad, you seem in a hurry to leave." He pulled her into the curve of his arm. "I'll make breakfast. It's Saturday and we have the whole weekend ahead of us. How would you like to spend it?"

"Don't tempt me." She kissed him lightly. "A detective working on a case can't afford to think in terms of free weekends." She hoped she sounded sincere. Nothing would have pleased her more than to spend Saturday and Sunday with him, yet she held back. He had made it clear that he was avoiding commitments and she had announced that she didn't want to be involved in a relationship at this time. Yet when she slept with a man she tended to feel involved. Deeply involved. Rex's lovemaking, his total approval, affected her like a narcotic. She wanted more. Before she became totally hooked, she needed to distance herself from him — to be on guard. Her life had changed and she wasn't sure she liked the direction it had taken.

She dressed quickly as he watched from his cocoon of blankets, then he rose.

"I'll drive you home."

"Let me walk. I need to walk." She kissed him and tried to leave, but he held her.

"Have dinner with me tonight?"

"It's a deal. I'll cook the grouper." She kissed him once again, then let herself out of the house. He didn't stop her. The short walk through the gusting wind refreshed her, and nobody noticed her quiet entry into her apartment. The children were watching TV cartoons, and she heard Randy and Diane talking in the kitchen.

She had barely reached her room, showered, and changed into fresh clothing when her telephone rang.

"Dear child, I need to talk to you right away. Could you run over for a cup of coffee?"

"Of course, Beck. What's up?"

"Tell you when you get here. The coffee's on."

Katie ran a comb through her hair, grabbed her shoulder bag, and left the apartment as quietly as she had entered, walking through the garden gate to Hibiscus House where Beck waited in the doorway.

"Hope I didn't waken you." Beck thrust her hands deeply into the pockets of her lavender jumpsuit as she watched Katie climb the steps to the porch.

"I'm an early riser." She felt her face flush. Had Beck called earlier? Had she seen her come in just now? No matter. "What's the big news? Have you learned something important about the case?"

"Perhaps." Beck led her to the kitchen and they sat at a round oak table next to an industrial-sized stove. "Weather's not fit for a sea urchin today, but it's cozy in here. My cooks won't arrive for an hour or so." She poured their coffee from a blue china pot then offered Katie a pineapple-filled sweet roll.

"Just coffee, thanks." Katie sipped the brew and felt herself gradually coming to life.

"Katie, didn't you tell me that Elizabeth Wright was in Naples on business at the time of Alexa's murder?"

"Yes. That's what Elizabeth told me — that she left on that Monday morning and didn't return until Tuesday afternoon. I checked with Mac's friend at the airport. He confirmed her story from airport records."

"That's very strange. I talked again with Angie. I had mentioned nothing about Elizabeth Wright. We were discussing Angie's visit to Miami."

"Recent visit?" Katie asked, puzzled as to where the conversation was heading.

"On the morning of Alexa's murder, Angie was in Miami seeing a gynecologist. She suspected she was pregnant so she avoided visiting a local doctor. In this town nothing stays a secret very long."

"Nothing except the identity of Alexa's murderer." She cupped her hands around her coffee cup, enjoying its warmth.

"Angie was embarrassed because she almost ran face-to-face into Elizabeth Wright in Miami."

"Where did they meet? A gynecologist's office? Elizabeth's not preg . . ."

260

"They didn't exactly meet. Angie stepped into a bank to write a check so she could pay the gynecologist in cash, and she saw Elizabeth in the bank lobby. She recognized her because she had waited on her many times — sometimes here at Hibiscus House and sometimes at Rico's. She didn't think Elizabeth would recognize or remember her, but she wasn't sure."

"Then they didn't speak."

"No. Angie ducked from Elizabeth's sight, got her cash, and left the bank."

"Interesting." Katie sipped her coffee. "Wright buys a round trip ticket to Naples, yet she's seen in Miami."

"Why?" Beck poured them more coffee. "If she was going to Miami, why wouldn't she have bought a ticket to Miami?"

"Good question. Why? I've kept her on my list, and I'll look into this bit of subterfuge — if that's what it is."

"Your list?"

"The list of suspects you suggested I make."

Beck laughed. "I'd forgotten all about that."

"Well I did make a list and Wright was on it. Her alibi seemed convincing on the surface, and airport officials corroborated it, yet something about her puzzles me. I feel warning vibes every time I think of her."

"And now this."

"Yes. And now this. Thanks for telling me about Angie's experience. Wright may have flown to and from Naples as she claims, but she could have rented a car in Naples and driven to Miami. In fact, now that I think about it, she could have driven to Key West from Naples or from Miami, killed Alexa, driven back to Naples, and caught her scheduled flight home."

"Could you ever prove she did that?"

"With a lot of leg work, I might be able to. I'd have to go to Naples and talk with car rental people. They keep careful records. If Wright rented a car, there's a record of it somewhere."

"Could she have used a phony name?"

"Anything's possible. It's easy to get fake IDs."

"She could have borrowed a car from a friend," Beck said.

"That would be harder to check on."

"Will you try?"

"I don't know yet, but several things about Elizabeth Wright don't ring true. I'm not through thinking about her and about what bearing she may have on the Chitting case."

"Care to elaborate?"

"Not just yet, but you've given me fresh facts to think about. Sometimes plugging into another person's thinking helps me see the fallacies in my own reasoning."

"You miss your partner, don't you?"

"Yes. We bounce ideas off each other when we're on a case, but I'd really like to solve Alexa's murder on my own."

"Success builds confidence. Why not tell me your thoughts about Elizabeth Wright?

I'll try to be impartial, but frankly there's something about that woman I detest."

"She won't let me see any of the documents concerning the Cayo Hueso project. They're public information, yet I can't get to see them and that stinks."

"What reason does she give?"

"First she said they were in Tallahassee, but when I called that office they said copies of the documents were in Key West. When I confronted her with that information, she made a pretense of having her secretary search for the file, but of course it was missing. The secretary seemed genuinely surprised, but Elizabeth didn't."

"A file missing right when it's needed. Some coincidence."

"Yeah. For some reason she's withholding that file. And she acts smug about it, too."

"Why wouldn't she want you to see it?"

"Good question. I'm certainly no expert on blueprints or contracts."

"Maybe she resents your friendship with Rex. Being difficult could be her way of getting even."

"She may be using the file as a red herring. Maybe she's flaunting her authority to try to keep my attention focused on those papers so I'll overlook something else that's far more important to the Chitting case."

"That's an interesting thought. What did you hope to find in the documents?"

"I don't know. Sometimes a detective never knows what he's interested in until he sees it. But since that housing project loomed uppermost in Alexa Chitting's thinking, I thought the papers might in some way reveal clues that could lead to her murderer." Katie eased her chair from the table and stood.

"There's still more coffee."

"Thanks, but I must go. I appreciate your sharing this information. I feel sure that it fits into this tangle somewhere. Now I have to figure out where."

"You're welcome, dear child." Beck followed Katie to the steps. "Let me know how your investigation progresses."

"I will."

Instead of going home, Katie jogged through the chilly morning to her office. Beck's story galvanized her into action. Elizabeth Wright's alibi sucked. Her refusal to relinquish the Cayo Hueso file not only piqued Katie's curiosity, but it also rekindled her anger. She prepared to take action that could either fast forward her investigation or cause her a multiplicity of police problems.

Saturday. A good time for breaking and entering. The Office of Community Affairs would be closed for the weekend. She tucked her picklocks, miniature tape recorder, and the tiny camera she used for photographing documents into her shoulder bag and headed for Simonton Street.

Chapter Twenty-Five

She had jogged only a block or so when she paused, then backtracked to Flagler Avenue and headed north toward the Salvation Army Store. The thought of breaking and entering in the daylight flashed caution signals in her mind although she knew the police would be concentrating most of their activities on Front Street and Mallory Square, watching the traffic as tourists took to their cars to avoid the abrasive wind. Cops would give scant attention to Simonton Street offices until darkness made them fair game for druggies needing some bucks for the crack house.

She needed a lower profile. The police knew her by sight. She wore khaki shirts and skirts like a uniform during working hours, and blonde hair attracted attention. Someone on the force might even be following her. She regretted having gone to the department to talk with Lt. Brewer. If he thought she was trying to make trouble for his son over the bridge accident, he might try to retaliate.

As she entered the thrift shop, where several women were looking through the dresses on a circular rack just inside the front door, she planned her disguise. Why was she feeling like a nervous Nellie? Nobody was watching her. The building held the stale air and heat of previous days, maybe even previous months, and she wiped perspiration from her upper lip. To her left, a clerk rang up a sale then stuffed a pair of scuffed Wrights and a silk designer tie into a plain brown bag for an unshaven man wearing faded red sweats.

She reflected on the man's epicurean taste as she walked to a wall where headgear was displayed on aluminum hooks that protruded from a pegboard. She chose a navy and white babushka, then moved on to a rack of sport clothes where she selected an ankle-length jeans skirt and jacket. Completing the outfit with a white tank top, she carried the clothes to a makeshift dressing room at the back of the store and tried them on under the glare of a bare bulb suspended from a ceiling cord.

"Close enough," she muttered, checking the fit in a crazed wall mirror hanging in a baroque frame.

She slipped back into her own clothing and carried her new outfit to the checkout clerk.

"Will this be all, miss?" The woman rang up the sale.

"Yes. Thank you."

"That'll be three dollars and fifty cents, please."

She paid for the clothes and carried them toward the store entrance, waiting until another customer held the clerk's attention before she slipped back to the dressing room and changed into the disguise. Tucking her hair under the babushka, she put on her sunglasses. Even Bubba wouldn't recognize her in this outfit. She folded her khaki clothes, placed them in the brown sack, and left the store, stopping at her office long enough to leave the sack on her desk.

Once again she headed toward Simonton Street, buttoning her jacket as she fought the wind. When she reached the sea-green cottage that housed the Office of Community Affairs, she approached the entry and tried the door. No point in breaking in if some feckless employee might have accidentally left the door unlocked.

No such luck. She knocked three times to make sure nobody was inside.

"That office be closed on Satiddays, Ma'am," a woman called from across the street. "No open again until the Monday morning."

"Thank you," she called to the woman, then she searched in her shoulder bag for pen and paper and pretended to write a note which she stuck in the screen door. By the time she finished, the woman was hurrying on down the street, her head lowered into the wind.

Katie left the office's front entrance, walking along the side of the building to the back door, snagging her skirt on thorny bougainvillea, and watching carefully for anyone who might be observing her. She saw nobody. A high fence much like the one around Rex's tropical garden offered the privacy she needed and she pulled out her picklocks.

Her first and second attempts to open the lock failed, but on the third try, the mechanism gave way to her manipulations and she entered the office, closing the door behind her. It was that easy. Mac would have been proud of her B and E expertise.

At one time the structure had been a shotgun house, built with a long hallway separating the front and back doors and with small rooms opening off each side of the corridor. She followed the narrow passage to the front office where shades had been drawn for the weekend. Good. Although she moved about the premises without fear of detection from anyone passing by outside, her hands began to sweat. She wiped her palms on her skirt.

Methodical. She had to be methodical. Check the file cabinets first. She approached the steel files behind the secretary's desk, opening the top drawer and searching the folders quickly.

"Cayo Hueso. Not here." She checked every folder to make sure she hadn't overlooked the Cayo Hueso papers. Miss Scarlet Fingernails hadn't lied. The folder wasn't in the file. As her gaze fell on the secretary's desk, she moved to it and began checking its drawers. Letterheads. Envelopes. Stamps. Computer paper. The bottom drawer held a half-filled bottle of gin, an almost empty bottle of tonic water, and three paperback romances. Telling details. She always found another person's choice of reading material fascinating.

Perhaps Wright had hidden the file in her private office. Katie entered that room, again tripping slightly on the rattan rug and touching the doorjamb for support.

"You should get that rug fixed, Liz. Tacky really isn't your style."

She stood in the doorway studying the office. A former bedroom? That would account for the closet in the corner. Walking first to the oak desk, she paused. Had Wright left markers so she could tell later if her office had been disturbed? Katie examined the drawer openings for telltale bits of paper or fabric, but she found none. She began searching. The top drawer contained only ballpoints, paper clips, emery boards. She touched a bottle of nail gloss and a lipstick, noting the trendy shade and pricey brand.

The side drawers proved equally uninteresting: state department bulletins, manuals, an old newspaper. She jumped when the telephone rang. Who would be calling on Saturday? A wrong number, perhaps. Or had

Elizabeth Wright planned to be here to accept a call? That put her on guard. But unlikely. Wright wasn't the type to spend her weekends slaving for the State Department. The phone rang ten times. She didn't realize she had been holding her breath until the ringing stopped.

What if Elizabeth had been expecting a call? What if. What if. A growing sense of urgency made her hurry. The bottom desk drawer was locked, but after a few minutes it opened to her deft probing with a picklock. Bonanza. A red folder bearing the words CAYO HUESO PROJECT lay on top of some books. She laid the folder on the desk, pulled her special camera from her shoulder bag and began photographing the pages. Sketches. Contracts. Proposals. Letters. She had no time to read them now.

A burgeoning sense of impending danger made it hard for her to keep the camera steady, yet she must. Holding her breath while she clicked the shutter helped, but it also made her conscious of her jackhammer heart. Could Alexa Chitting's death in some way be connected with the information in these papers? Why else would Wright have denied her access to this folder and have locked it in her private desk? Again she paused to wipe her damp hands on her skirt.

It took several minutes to photograph every page of the file, and her hands were shaking as she started to replace the folder in the bottom drawer exactly as she had found it. Then she stopped, staring at the small books that had been lying under the file folder.

"Bank books. Blue. Red. Brown. So many of them." She counted eleven checking account books, then she examined them more closely. Each book showed a deposit of nine thousand dollars, made on the date of Alexa's murder.

"Ninety-nine thousand dollars," Katie muttered, sitting down in Elizabeth's desk chair as the full impact of this find hit her. One thousand dollars less than the amount Po said Alexa had withdrawn from her account just before her death.

She stacked the bankbooks in a neat pile and began examining each one again, muttering the bank names to herself. "Naples First National. Security Savings Bank of Naples. First Fidelity Bank. Miami Savings and Loan. Miami First National. Flagler Street Bank of Miami." Three of the banks were located in Naples and eight in Miami. All the books had been issued in Elizabeth Wright's name.

Picking up her camera, she photographed the first and only entry in each of the books. She was just replacing them in the bottom drawer when she heard a key scrape against the front door lock. Someone was coming.

A pulse hammered at her temple, her

throat as she looked around for a hiding place. It was too late to flee from the building. She heard the door lock turn, heard the door open.

Hide. Hide.

The kneehole of the desk?

The closet?

If the intruder was Elizabeth Wright, she would surely beeline to her desk. Katie opted for the closet. She opened the door, slipped inside, then left the door slightly ajar so she could watch a part of what went on in the room. The stuffy cubicle reeked of ammonia, sweeping compound, a lemon-scented dust cloth. What if she sneezed! What if the intruder came to the closet for something? She looked behind her, and now that her eyes had adjusted to the dimness, she could make out a carton of paper towels large enough to hide her if she hunkered and ducked her head. The thought offered slight comfort.

Again she jumped as the telephone rang. Now she saw Elizabeth Wright hurry to answer it, tripping slightly over the frayed carpet as she entered the room. Another time Katie might have laughed, but not today. She listened carefully, wishing she could reach her tape recorder without making any noise, but no way. Elizabeth stood too close to the closet door. She would hear the rustle of clothing, the shifting of weight on the old floorboards.

The conversation was meaningless — a series of yes and no answers on Wright's part. She replaced the receiver, then opened the top drawer of her desk and proceeded to write a note that she placed in the center of her blotter. Katie watched as Wright opened each side desk drawer, and again Katie held her breath. There had been no time to lock the bottom drawer. She never doubted that Wright would notice.

Katie watched. When the drawer glided open, she saw Wright's body stiffen.

"Who . . . ," the word escaped involuntarily. Wright counted the bankbooks, stuffed them into her shoulder bag, then re-locked the drawer.

Katie barely breathed, hoping Wright would take the books and leave. Instead, she turned and eyed the open closet door. Then she looked at her bottom desk drawer again. Katie could see Elizabeth Wright's hand tremble as she fumbled in her bag then pulled out a small gun, aiming it at the closet door.

"Who's in the closet? I know someone's there. Come out with your hands up."

Chapter Twenty-Six

When she saw the gun, Katie's mind flashed back to the classroom scene, to Jon McCartel, to another shooting. Fear turned her to stone. Trapped by her own foolishness! Why had she come here without telling someone where she would be? The locked drawer. The Cayo Hueso file. The bankbooks. They were adding up to her death. A gut feeling told her that Elizabeth Wright had murdered Alexa and that she wouldn't hesitate to kill again. It would be easier the second time.

"Come out with your hands up."

The low, deadly voice prompted Katie to squirm farther to the back of the closet where she crouched behind the carton of towels. She could no longer see the woman or the gun, but the floorboards creaked as footsteps approached, and light flooded in as Elizabeth Wright flung open the door and stepped inside the closet. Katie looked into the gun barrel.

"So it's you!" Contempt roughened Wright's voice and she backed into her office. "Get up!"

Katie stood.

"Place your hands on your head and come out of there."

Katie obeyed, standing just outside the closet door and feeling more vulnerable than she had felt in all her life.

"What are you doing here?"

"Looking for the Cayo Hueso file." She forced strength into her voice. "Those documents are public records and I have a legal right to see them. You're breaking the law by withholding them."

"And my office is private property. You've no legal right to be here. I'll call the police and have you arrested for trespassing, for breaking and entering, for . . . you . . . you scum. And you found the bankbooks too, didn't you?"

"Yes." No point in lying. "The arresting officers you plan to call will probably find the bankbooks most interesting. Where did all that money come from? That's the very first question they'll ask you. Where did it come from?"

"None of your business!" A flush flooded Wright's neck and rose to her hairline, making her face look drawn and raddled. "You've seen too much, Katie Hassworth, P.I." She steadied the gun with both hands.

"So before I die, tell me about the bankbooks." She forced bravado into her voice, but her arms were beginning to ache, and she had to fight to keep her body from shaking. Was the gun Elizabeth Wright held the same gun that had fired a shot into

Alexa's wall hanging?

"I'll tell you nothing." She reached for the telephone.

"The money came from Alexa Chitting, didn't it?"

Wright's lips parted, but she didn't answer.

"Don't look so surprised. Po told me that Alexa had withdrawn a hundred thou from her account the Friday before her death, receiving it in cash. But he didn't know what she had done with it."

"The Chitting affairs are none of my concern."

"Why did Alexa give you the hundred thou?"

"You don't know what you're talking about." Her voice sounded less sure. "Po Chitting knew nothing of his wife's business dealings."

"So you *were* concerned with Chitting affairs. You're contradicting yourself."

"It's common gossip that the Chittings didn't get along, that Alexa ran the marina."

"Po knew about the hundred thousand. Cash." Talk. Talk. She had to keep talking. Talk was her only defense. Her mouth felt so dry her lips threatened to stick to her teeth, but she forced more words. "Were you uneasy carrying so much cash? Where did you hide it over the weekend? It must have made some bundle! Did you sleep with it under your pillow?"

"You're in no position to question me!"

"Did one suitcase hold it? Two suitcases? It must have been some sort of a payoff."

"I'm going to shoot you."

"You'd be foolish to kill me here. I'm unarmed. You couldn't even plead self-defense. Insanity, maybe, but do you really want to do time in a mental ward? I've heard they're not a lot of fun."

"A person is allowed to defend himself and his property. You're an intruder on my premises." She raised the gun a fraction of an inch.

"You've a right to defend yourself, but not with undue force. Using a gun against an unarmed person will be considered undue force. Believe it. The police will. So will the jury of your peers."

"Well *I* don't believe it."

"Kill me and you'll do time. That's a promise. May I please lower my hands?"

Wright cleared her throat and shook her head as if Katie's words confused her. "Keep your hands where they are. You can't get away with this."

"And you can't get away with Alexa Chitting's murder."

Wright gave a harsh laugh. "What put that idea into your head! Alexa and I were involved in an important business transaction, but I certainly didn't kill her. Maybe you need to go back to detective school."

She wished she had been able to activate her tape recorder. Wright had just admitted to a business deal with Alexa, but she could deny it later. "Please, may I lower my hands? Your gun will keep you in control."

"All right, but one threatening move from you and I'll pull the trigger. Count on it."

Katie lowered her arms, feeling warmth return to her fingertips as the blood began circulating freely once more. In the strained quiet between them her mind began to clear, offering theories, possibilities. Talk. She had to keep Wright talking.

"The money was a bribe, wasn't it, Ms. Wright? Alexa was bribing you."

"Alexa was dying of cancer. The money was payment for a favor."

"Then it did come from Alexa. I thought so."

Wright's lips clamped into a tight white line as she realized she had confirmed information that Katie had only been surmising. "Of course I'll deny that if anyone questions me. It will be my word against yours."

"I can guess the nature of the favor," Katie said. "Suddenly you found the salt ponds totally inappropriate as a location for Cayo Hueso. Traffic would snarl. The population increase would have a negative impact on the environment. And what about the endangered alligators and egrets? Once you changed your position and vetoed using the salt ponds for the housing project, Alexa paid you the hundred grand."

"You're wrong, of course." Elizabeth chuckled. "Even if you lived to present your theory to the public, nobody would believe you. You seem to forget that in the last analysis, I was strongly in favor of the Cayo Hueso project being built in the salt pond area. The newspaper even carried that headline."

"But of course you were in favor of it once Alexa was dead. The public isn't totally dumb. People can figure out that you vetoed the salt pond area and accepted Alexa's bribe. Then you killed her and did another about-face. As the old cliché goes, you wanted to eat your cake and have it, too. And you almost succeeded."

"You're making no sense at all."

"By killing Alexa, you were then free to go ahead with Cayo Hueso at the salt pond location."

"You've got to be kidding."

"Only Alexa could have proved that you accepted a bribe. And she was dead. You hid the money carefully, depositing it in amounts that wouldn't draw undue attention from bank officials or the IRS. You were set, weren't you! You had a fortune, and you knew that the successful completion of the Cayo Hueso development would earn you a much coveted career advancement. You thought you had it all, didn't you?"

"Nobody will believe a tale like that. Not for a minute."

Katie kept talking. "Of course people will believe me. They can see that you'd not only have a nice cushion of Alexa's money plus the interest it had drawn, but you'd also have the Cayo Hueso project to your credit and a substantial raise in salary."

"You're not going to lay Alexa Chitting's murder at my doorstep!" Her tone grew low and menacing. "I didn't kill her and I won't let you botch my career by dragging my name through a lot of rotten publicity for the sake of your big detective ego. You're a dead woman."

"Think, Wright, think. You shoot me here and you'll have to hide my body. That won't be easy. Have you thought through that problem?"

"Hide your body! Are you crazy? I'll shoot you and call the police immediately. It's that simple. Self defense. No jury would blame me."

"An unarmed person attacking a person with a gun? Who'd buy that story!"

"Pick up a bookend from my desk."

Katie hesitated, eyeing the heavy brass sharks that supported several books.

"Pick one of them up. Grab it firmly. Get your fingerprints all over it."

Katie picked up the bookend, hearing the

soft thud of the books as they fell against the desk blotter. She tasted a bitterness on the back of her tongue. The taste of death?

"Now you have a weapon. I'll tell the police that you came at me with the bookend and I had to defend myself. When they see that shark, they'll believe me. A blow from it could be lethal."

"A gun against a bookend? The prosecuting attorney will call it undue force."

"So I panicked. Most policemen are chauvinists. Their upbringing has programmed them to expect women to panic. I'll be believed."

Katie knew those words were probably true. Now what! She had to act fast. In picking up the bookend, she had stepped closer to her foe. On impulse she gave Wright's wrist a sharp chop with the side of her hand which sent the gun flying across the carpet.

"You . . ." Wright gasped.

They both lunged for the gun. Wright's hand closed over it, but Katie slammed the bookend against her fingers, making her shriek and draw back. Before Katie could drop the bookend and grab the gun, Wright clutched it again. And it went off.

The bullet grazed Katie's arm as it tore through a shade and the windowpane. Clutching her arm, she froze, momentarily stunned as she felt warm blood on her fingers. Wright stood dazed by the sound, and Katie seized the chance to act. Ignoring the searing heat that flooded her left arm, she gave Wright's wrist another chop. This time Katie caught the gun as it fell.

"Hands on your head." Her voice came in short gasps and she aimed the gun at Wright as she raised her hands.

"You won't get by with this, Hassworth."

Katie eased to the desk, removed the telephone receiver with her left hand in spite of the pain and the blood running down her arm. With the receiver lying on the desk, she tried to call the police without looking away from her captive. Blood dripped on the desk blotter and her arm throbbed through a white searing numbness.

"Police department, Sgt. Babcock speaking."

The voice seemed to come from a great distance. Picking up the receiver with her numbed left hand, Katie had just started to speak when Wright kicked the gun from her hand, then raced for the door.

"Stop!" Retrieving the gun, Katie fired into the air, but Wright continued to run, heading for Duval Street and its many hole-in-the-wall shops.

Katie lowered the gun and gave her message to the police.

"Katie Hassworth speaking from the Simonton Street Office of Community Affairs. There's been a shooting."

Chapter Twenty-Seven

By the time the police arrived, Katie had managed to grab paper towels to stay the flow of blood, and fighting a nauseating dizziness, she walked to the door to greet the officers.

"I believe we've met before, Miss Hassworth. I'm Sgt. Babcock and this is my partner, Sgt. La Rosa. Are you all right?" He tossed his brown cigarette onto the doorstep and ground it out with his toe before he entered the office.

She looked up at Babcock as she nodded her acknowledgment of the greeting, then her eyes met those of the paunchy Cuban officer on a level. "I'm all right. The bullet just grazed my arm."

"Who shot you?" Babcock's eyes looked like flint as he studied the bloodstains on the desk blotter, the telephone, the gun.

"Elizabeth Wright shot me and she's escaping." She nodded toward Duval Street. "She headed that way, and she's wearing gray sweats and jogging shoes, but she may have a car around here somewhere."

"We'll drive you to the emergency room," Babcock said.

"I'm fine!" She heard herself shouting.

"Get Elizabeth Wright. I think she murdered Alexa Chitting."

Sgt. Babcock raised his eyebrows. Sgt. La Rosa patted his paunch and asked, "Why do you think that, Ma'am?"

La Rosa's patronizing tone infuriated her, but she forced herself to be calm as she blurted her story about seeing the bankbooks, about Wright holding her at gunpoint, about accusing Wright of accepting a bribe. She avoided mentioning the fact that she had picked the lock to gain entry to the office. Plenty of time for Wright to report that after her capture.

"Where are the bank books now?" Sgt. Babcock asked.

"In her shoulder bag. Go after her!"

"Ninety-nine thousand big ones!" Sgt. La Rosa said. "Holey moley."

"Almost the exact amount that Po Chitting told me Alexa had withdrawn from her account the Friday before she died." She spoke in a rush, hoping to make the men realize the need for action. "Elizabeth took Alexa's bribe, nixed the salt pond area for the Cayo Hueso project, murdered Alexa, then supported the salt pond location again once Alexa wasn't around to protest."

"Miss Wright admitted that the money came from Alexa Chitting?" Babcock lit another brown cigarette.

"Yes. She said they had a business deal. I

guessed the kind of deal."

"But there are holes in your theory, Miss Hassworth." Babcock's voice took on an avuncular and patronizing tone as he said her name. "Perhaps you're right about the bribe. We'll check into that once we talk with Miss Wright. But you have no proof that she murdered Mrs. Chitting."

"It figures." She winced as her arm throbbed.

"In your mind, it may figure." Babcock shook his head. "But *figuring* won't stand up in court. It's more formally known as conjecture. You're back to square one. Anyone could have wasted Alexa Chitting. Perhaps Miss Wright took a bribe. And she may have used the coincidental murder to her advantage. We'll consider that theory when we talk with her."

"You'll never get to talk with her if you don't apprehend her." Frustration left Katie weak. Or maybe it was the loss of blood. "Elizabeth Wright shot me. Aren't you going to do something about that?" She loosened that paper towel she had been holding against her wound and blood flowed again.

"Why did she shoot you?" Babcock asked.

"Because I accused her of murder."

"Not very bright of you," La Rosa said. "Didn't you know she had a gun?"

"I knew it." She told them of the struggle over the gun. "Both our prints are on the gun. And on the bookend. I suppose you'll try to prove that I grabbed her gun and shot myself."

"I suppose that could be a possibility," Babcock said, "now that you mention it. We'll consider that theory after we take you to the hospital."

"I'm fine! Catch Elizabeth Wright, then worry about me and the hospital. She could be escaping right this minute."

"Escaping to where?" La Rosa asked. "You forget that we're on an island that's just one of a long chain of islands. There are a limited amount of places where a fugitive can hide."

"She could board a plane or a boat. She might even . . ."

"La Rosa," Babcock said. "Get on the radio. Order our men to stop Elizabeth Wright for questioning."

La Rosa patted his paunch thoughtfully before he left the office and strolled toward the patrol car parked at the curb. Katie knew he was trying to infuriate her with his slowness. He succeeded.

"Collect your things," Sgt. Babcock said. "We're going to the emergency room. Where's your car?"

"It's at my office, and I have no things to collect."

"Then let's go."

Although Sgt. Babcock sounded the siren

to clear traffic, few cars pulled over. In some cases radios blared hard rock that drowned out the siren's wail. In other instances, there was no place to pull over. She felt a greater danger in the speeding patrol car than she had felt as Elizabeth Wright's captive.

Once they entered the hospital, she grew faint. Memories of another shooting, another wound, replayed through her mind. Green walls. Tan floors. The swish of white uniforms. Did all hospitals look and sound alike? The medicinal smell brought an acrid taste to her mouth.

Sgt. Babcock spoke to the nurse at the emergency room desk and she beeped a doctor, then led Katie to an examining room that majored in fluorescent lights, white porcelain, and stainless steel.

After a lengthy wait, a portly doctor arrived, stethoscope dangling around his neck, white coat unbuttoned to reveal a red tank top bearing the logo, Conch Republic. He looked like the type who might have seceded from the union years ago.

"It's a superficial wound." The doctor probed, cleansed, applied medicine. "Won't even need stitches." A nurse offered a tray of bandages, and he selected the ones he needed, applying them to the cleaned wound. "You'll be as good as new in a few days."

"Thank you, Doctor." As she stood to leave, the room did a slow spiral and she felt herself falling into a vortex of darkness. When she opened her eyes again, it took her a few moments to figure out that she was in a hospital bed and a hospital gown. It took her another moment to realize that it was now growing dark outside and that a uniformed officer sat patting his paunchy stomach just outside her door. Her arm ached.

"La Rosa?" she called.

Sgt. La Rosa stood and approached her bed. "Ah, so you're awake. I'll call the nurse."

The nurse appeared before La Rosa could call. "You're feeling better, Miss Hassworth?"

"I'm fine." She pushed herself up in bed, looking about for her clothes as she tried to swing her legs over the side of the mattress. "I'm going home now."

"I'm afraid you can't leave until morning," the nurse said. "Doctor's orders. You've lost quite a bit of blood and he wants to monitor your vital signs for several hours before dismissing you. I'll bring you some juice."

"What are you doing here?" Katie asked La Rosa as the nurse padded away on her ripple-soled shoes.

"I'm here to guard you."

"I don't want a guard."

"I've got my orders."

"I don't want a guard. Get out!"

"Your life was endangered. You'll be under

guard until your assailant is apprehended."

"Elizabeth Wright. She's still on the run? What are you guys doing — standing on your shoestrings?"

"These things sometimes take time. We'll get her. We've set up a roadblock at the Boca Chica Bridge."

"She did the shooting, but I'm the one who's a prisoner. Unfair." She eased from the bed, found her disguise in the closet along with a hospital robe, which she slipped on. When the nurse returned, Katie confronted her.

"I want to go home. Now."

"I'm afraid that's impossible. I've told you. Doctor's orders. I've no authority to dismiss you."

"May I make a telephone call? Prisoners are allowed one call."

"You're not a prisoner, Miss Hassworth." The nurse's voice grew testy and even more patronizing. "There's a telephone by your bed. You may make as many calls as you care to. You may be up and about, if you feel able." She set the glass of juice on the bed-side table and swished from the room.

Katie glared after her, then turned the glare on La Rosa. "I'd like to make my call in private, please."

"Excuse me, Ma'am." He retreated to his chair outside her door, but she knew he would eavesdrop. She would have done the

289

same thing had their positions been reversed.

She punched out Diane's number. No response. Then she tried Rex, suddenly remembering their dinner date. He answered on the second ring.

"Katie! Where are you? When you weren't at home when I got there, I drove by your office. And there was your car, but no Katie. I've been calling your office and your apartment every five minutes. I was about to go to the police."

She blinked back a rush of tears as she realized how much his concern touched her. "Oh, Rex. I'm sorry I've put you through a bad time."

"You've been in danger ever since you took the Chitting case and it drives me wild. Are you okay? What's been going on? Where are you?"

She related her whereabouts, her story of the shooting, her theories concerning Elizabeth Wright.

"Are you sure you're all right?"

She heard concern strain his voice. "I'm fine. I'm just furious that they're keeping me here all night — and under guard at that."

"The guard's for your protection."

"So they say. I have no clear picture of Elizabeth Wright sneaking in to shoot me in my bed. My guess is that she's well on her way to Miami — or somewhere. I want out of here."

"I'll be right there," Rex said. "Maybe

they'll let you go for a walk if you feel up to it. I'll bring you a sweater."

"It's colder?"

"This front is really letting us have it. Maybe you'd prefer staying inside — even if it's inside a hospital."

"Thanks, Rex. I'd love to see you. Maybe you can reason with Lady Godzilla and spring me from this place."

Before Rex arrived, a nurse served a light supper, and Katie ate every bit of it to prove that she was well and feeling fine and could just as well be home.

When Rex arrived, he carried something in a nest of tissue paper. "Flower shops are closed, so I picked this up from a vendor at Mallory. The street types don't gift wrap."

She smiled at him as she unwrapped a polished scallop shell hanging from a silken cord. "A necklace! It's lovely, Rex. Thank you." She allowed him to slip it over her head and around her neck, conscious all the while of the observing eyes of Sgt. La Rosa.

"You can go out for a walk," Rex said. "I asked at the nurse's station. All you have to do is sign a checkout sheet. We can find a place that's protected from the wind."

She signed out, Rex slipped a sweater around her shoulders, and they left the hospital. The cool air felt invigorating after the warmth of her room, and they had almost circled the building before she noticed La

Rosa trailing them at a discreet distance, head drawn into his jacket like a turtle.

"No privacy," she said. "No privacy at all."

"Who needs privacy?" Rex pulled her into a sheltered ell then wrapped her in his warm embrace, taking care not to hurt her injured arm. They kissed deeply, molding their bodies together as they relaxed against each other, unmindful of the cold.

"Katie. Katie. I was so worried about you. You could have been killed."

"Elizabeth is a rotten shot."

"I'm glad." He kissed her again. "Look, when you get out of here, we'll celebrate the fact that you're still alive."

"I'm getting out tomorrow morning. I won't let them hold me any longer."

"Where's your car?"

"At home."

"Give me the key and I'll leave it in the hospital lot for you. Or maybe I should pick you up and drive you home."

"I don't know what time they'll spring me. You know doctors! I'd really appreciate knowing that my car is here."

"Done. Then we'll have lunch at my house. Your choice of menu. What'll it be? I'll cook."

"How about conch chowder and onion rolls?"

"It's a deal."

Chapter Twenty-Eight

On Sunday morning Katie had a slight temperature and the doctor delayed her dismissal for another day. She called Rex with the wretched news.

"I'm sorry, Katie. But I'm glad they're taking good care of you."

"But our lunch . . . I want out of here."

"I would have had to cancel anyway. Dad phoned from New York. I have to fly up this morning and . . . talk about a business deal. Let's make it dinner tomorrow night. I'll be back sometime late afternoon and I know you'll have been dismissed by then."

She sighed deeply. "Fine. Have a good flight."

"Oh, by the way. Diane will park your car near the back door of the hospital and bring the keys up to you. I'd do it myself, but I'm catching an early flight."

"You're a doll. Take care in New York." She eyed his sweater lying on her bedside chair. She would take it to him tomorrow.

A day. A whole day to hang around the hospital with nothing to do. Although cold wind still chilled the island, Diane arrived with a garden bouquet and her car keys during afternoon visiting hours. Beck Dixon telephoned to wish her well. Babcock relieved La Rosa, and they played gin in the late afternoon. Babcock won.

Elizabeth Wright still roamed at large. The fact made Katie uneasy. She retired early, but she lay thinking, thinking. If the police were right, if Wright hadn't murdered Alexa Chitting, then who had? Reluctantly she admitted that she lacked the facts necessary to prove her case against Wright. Her evidence was circumstantial, merely conjecture.

She ran the suspects and their alibis through her mind once again, like the credits at the end of a movie, trying to remember what each person had said, how each had acted. Po. If he had been able to slip from the bar to deliver a rosebud, he could also have taken time to kill Alexa. Randy Dade. Maybe the bridge accident hadn't delayed him as long as he said. Mary Bethel. She had a key to Alexa's office. She had no strong alibi. Shadows against a window shade would count for little in the eyes of a prosecuting attorney.

She let her attention linger on Mary. She could have returned to the marina and entered Alexa's office unquestioned by the dockmasters or by Alexa. Nobody would have been surprised to see her there. But she had no proof that Mary had returned to the marina that night. None at all.

When she thought of Tyler Parish, she shuddered. Having a guard at her door didn't seem like such a bad idea after all. Parish scared her. She needed to know more about him. Who were his friends? Where did he hang out in his spare time? Maybe Bubba could help her with those details.

She felt chilly as a grim thought knifed through her mind and a cold rain pounded against her windowpane. She remembered how hot she had been hiding in Elizabeth Wright's closet and wished she had some of that warmth now. Sitting up, she reached for the blanket on the foot of her bed and pulled it over her shoulders. How good it felt.

A nurse opened her door, and a shaft of light from the hallway fell on the chair where Rex's sweater lay — the same sweater she had worn beside his pool, the same sweater she had worn on their walk around the hospital grounds, and the same sweater she had worn the night a wave had drenched them on the pier.

As she thought of the cold outside and the warmth of the sweater, a hunch flashed into her mind. A sweater. The hunch grew into a revelation. She sat up and pounded her pillow. How had she missed it before? She forgot about Tyler Parish and concentrated on the sweater and on the bullet in the wall hanging and on the conch shell that had announced Alexa Chitting's birth — and her death. She knew what she had to do the minute the doctor dismissed her from the hospital. Mentally she thanked Diane for bringing her car to the back door.

To her surprise she slept well that night. She rose early the next morning. Her arm still hurt, but her mind blanked out the pain as she began to put her plan into effect. Sometime during the night, the guard had changed. La Rosa sat outside her room. She closed the door and dressed in the denim outfit, wishing she had her khaki clothes instead. This time she carefully fastened the miniature tape recorder to her bra. When she opened her door again, she heard a news announcer's voice drone from La Rosa's radio.

". . . Elizabeth Wright has been apprehended in the alleged shooting of Detective Kathleen Hassworth."

La Rosa snapped off the radio and looked at her. "As soon as you're dismissed, I've orders to escort you to headquarters."

"The idea gives me a real thrill." She had to act quickly. Now would be her only chance. If she waited, Mac would return to find the Chitting case still unsolved and to find her in jail on Elizabeth Wright's B and E charge. She couldn't face such ignominious failure. She knew who had killed Alexa Chitting, but again her evidence was circumstantial. She had to get a confession if she hoped to put the murderer behind bars.

Finding ballpoint and paper in her shoulder bag, she wrote a note to La Rosa, dropped it into her skirt pocket, then laid her bag on the bedside chair. She waited. During the heightened activity in the hallway when the nurses changed shifts, she approached the sergeant, smiling and jingling some coins.

"I'm dying for coffee." She thrust the money at him. "Would you get me a cup? There's a machine downstairs in the family waiting room."

La Rosa yawned and patted his paunch. "All right. I could use a cup, too."

"I've got more change." She shook more coins from her purse. "Be my guest."

Once the elevator door closed behind La Rosa, she snapped on the bathroom light, turned on a faucet, then closed the door. How long would it take someone to realize she wasn't inside washing up? She draped Rex's sweater over her arm, hid her bag under it, and slipped from the room. Avoiding the elevator across from the nurses' station, she dashed down the stairway at the other end of the hall, then forced herself to walk as she left the building. Once outside, she ran to the police car parked at the curb and stuck her note to La Rosa under the windshield wiper before she sprinted to her own car and drove to her office.

Her key jammed in the lock and she swore as she removed it and reinserted it more carefully. Racing to her file cabinet, she unlocked the bottom drawer and grabbed her gun, loaded it, and dropped it into her skirt pocket. Guns. She hated them.

Had La Rosa missed her yet? She needed time. Dashing back to her car, she drove to Chitting Marina and took the elevator to Alexa's former office. Good. Mary Bethel was there. Katie activated her tape recorder then knocked.

"Katie Hassworth, Mary."

"Come in."

Katie opened the door and faced Mary, who rose from her chair looking both surprised and irritated. "It's all over, Mary. The police will be here in a few minutes." She slipped one hand into her skirt pocket, gripping her gun. What if she was wrong about Mary? She had been wrong about Elizabeth.

"Why are you barging in here this way? What are you talking about? You owe me an explanation."

"I'm talking about Alexa Chitting's murder. I've just remembered what it was about your story that rang false. You killed her, didn't you?"

"You're out of your mind. Of course I didn't kill her. You heard my alibi. You talked with Maria Gonzales. She and Mrs. Abresco saw me at home that night. They told me you talked with them. Don't be tedious. I'm very busy this morning."

"They saw your shadow. They didn't see you because you weren't there. You wear a wig, don't you?"

As if by reflex, Mary's hand flew to her hair and she flushed.

"Don't deny it. In all our wind and humidity, it's impossible to keep natural hair looking as perfect as yours always looks."

"What does my hair have to do with Alexa's death?" She reached for the telephone. "I'm calling the dockmaster's office to have you removed from the premises."

Katie shoved the telephone aside. "Hear me out. The police are on their way, but I want your full confession before they arrive."

"Confession! I'll confess to nothing. I'll call my lawyer. I'll . . ."

"You arranged your desk chair at home to look as if you were sitting in it, placing your wig form on it and focusing the lamplight in a way that cast a shadow onto the window shade. Maria Gonzales assumed the shadow was you. But it wasn't. You were here in this office bludgeoning Alexa with a conch shell."

"That's a lie." Her voice rose in pitch and volume. "You can never prove such a thing."

"Your line about the sweater gave you away."

"The sweater?" Mary gripped the edge of her desk, and Katie saw her knuckles grow white.

"When I asked you when you last saw

Alexa alive, you said you saw her as you left work. You told me that you slipped on your sweater and walked out the door. Those were your exact words."

"That's right. That's what I did."

"That may have been what you did, but you didn't do it at five o'clock. You did it *later* that Monday night. Think back. Alexa died the night a cold front numbed the island. But that *day* Po Chitting took his grandkids swimming in the afternoon because it was so hot. It was no day for wearing sweaters at five o'clock. But that night the cold front hit. The locals bee-lined to Captain Tony's fireplace."

"Many times I feel a chill. The temperature frequently fluctuates in January."

"But on the night Alexa died, the temperature drop came long after dark. I'm guessing that you always kept a sweater on hand here. You must have come back to the office that night, arriving in your street clothes in order not to arouse suspicion, and then changing into a dockmaster's uniform and the wasp mask in the elevator. After you murdered Alexa, you washed up and changed back into your street clothes. Then . . ."

"I don't know what you're talking about. I've never worn a dockmaster's uniform or a mask."

"I'm guessing you murdered Alexa then shucked out of the uniform and left it for the police to find. Why not? Lots of people had access to dockmaster uniforms. You changed into your street clothes which you probably had left on the balcony, then you grabbed your sweater."

"No. No . . ."

"The dockmaster uniform must have been blood-soaked. That's why you wore a disguise, isn't it? Not only would it frighten Alexa, but it would also keep blood splatters off your own clothing. I'm sure you washed up in the bathroom, but are you positive you didn't spatter some of Alexa's blood on that sweater? On your street clothes? The police will want to check on that."

"Get out of here!"

"You still have those things, don't you? Your frugal habits wouldn't allow you to throw out a perfectly good dress or sweater. Just one drop of blood on them that matches Alexa's could convict you. By using DNA testing, the police can identify blood samples accurately."

In the next instant, Mary jerked open her desk drawer and reached for her gun.

"Don't do that." Katie aimed her pistol, holding it steady in spite of her fear and the burning ache in her arm. "Drop it and get your hands up."

The gun thunked onto the desk, and Mary raised her hands. Where was La Rosa? Surely he had found her message by now. She wasn't going to repeat her mistake of trying to dial the phone and keep her suspect covered at the same time. Talk. The police would arrive. Talk. Get the confession.

"You killed Alexa to insure your annual stipend, didn't you?"

No response.

"Was fifty thousand a year worth a human life — the life of a friend who cared for you, educated you, provided you with employment?"

Suddenly Mary's face twisted into a snarl. "She *owed* me. Alexa only cared about Alexa. She never cared about me. Nobody has ever really cared for me. All through my childhood I was the kid with no parents — the kid who was different, and it was all Alexa's fault. I hated her."

"And so you killed her."

"Why shouldn't I hate her? She killed my parents and went scot-free. Everything she did for me was to assuage her guilty conscience. Her new will would have taken away my inheritance. Don't you understand? She *owed* me that money."

"So you killed her, right?"

"I hated her guts. I hated being her servant — for that's all I was to her — a servant. I did her personal chores. I even shopped for the elegant lingerie she wore on her evenings with Tyler. She deserved to die. *She owed me,* and I killed her."

Mary paused, and Katie prayed that her recorder was working. The confession! She had it! She felt her heart pound as she sought more information. "And you tried to implicate Po by planting his jacket button at the murder scene."

"She expected me to track down replacement buttons in some obscure shop in Rome. It would have meant giving up good writing time to find a button! And she *expected* it of me."

"You're such a small person, Mary. I wondered how you could have overcome Alexa with the conch, but it was easy, wasn't it? First you held her at gunpoint. There was no way she could defend herself against your gun. The shot that went wild probably scared her into submission."

"How did you know?"

Keeping her gun aimed at Mary, Katie backed to the wall near Alexa's desk. Lifting one corner of the Oriental hanging, she touched the bullet the police had overlooked. "After your gunshot frightened her, you had her where you wanted her, didn't you? You grabbed the conch to finish the job."

Before Mary could reply, Babcock and La Rosa rushed through the doorway, guns at the ready. Katie turned her head, and in that moment of confusion, Mary grabbed her gun and dropped down behind her desk.

"She's armed," Katie shouted. "She'll shoot."

303

"Stand back," Babcock ordered Katie.

La Rosa rushed forward, planting himself between Katie and Mary's desk while Babcock quietly circled behind the desk.

"Raise your hands and stand up," La Rosa said. "Now!"

In the next instant Mary jumped up, her gun aimed at La Rosa, but before she could shoot, Babcock kicked the desk chair into her backside. As she lost her balance, he circled his left arm around her neck and grabbed her right wrist with his right hand, squeezing until her fingers relaxed and the gun fell to the carpet.

"And there you have Alexa Chitting's murderer," Katie said, still aiming her gun at Mary.

"She's confessed?" Sgt. Babcock asked.

"Yes," Katie said.

"I've confessed to nothing," Mary said.

"I've recorded her words on my mini-tape."

"They won't be admissible in court," Mary said. "Never."

Katie knew that was true, but she also knew the police would listen to the tape, that it would color their thinking and help direct their line of questioning. "Mary tried to pull her gun on me when I mentioned that Alexa's blood might be on her sweater — the sweater she wore that night of the murder. And I think you'll find that her gun's the same gun that fired a bullet into the Oriental carpet hanging behind Alexa's desk. The bullet's still there so you can check it out. Mary fired a shot to intimidate Alexa so she could use the conch shell to kill her."

Babcock picked up the gun from Mary's desk. "You may lower your hands, Miss Bethel. Anything you say now may be held against you. You have the right to remain silent and refuse to answer questions. Anything you say may be used against you in a court of law. We'll need a statement from you, Miss Hassworth, and we'll take you to headquarters for that."

Chapter Twenty-Nine

After a long question-and-answer session at police headquarters, the officers held Elizabeth Wright on bribery as well as assault and battery charges, and Mary Bethel for murder. They booked Katie for breaking and entering, then released her on her own recognizance. Katie drove to her office and locked her gun in the file drawer, then changed into her working clothes before leaving a note for Mac that gave the highlights of the Chitting case along with a phone number where she could be reached.

Relief. Elation. Sadness. She couldn't analyze all the feelings welling inside her. Enough time for that later. And plenty of time later for talking with the Chitting family, with Beck Dixon. The wind was dying down and the sun was breaking through the cloud cover as she drove to Rex's house, picked the lock, and entered.

"Some people never learn." She dropped her picklock back into her purse.

The makings for the conch chowder were in the refrigerator, and by the time Rex returned, the spicy aroma of the thick soup filled the house.

"Katie!" Rex called from the front doorway, then he hurried to the kitchen and swooped her into his arms, pressing her against him as his lips met hers. Moments later he stood back to look at her. "I heard the news on the radio as I drove from the airport. Big congratulations! Tell me all about it. I want to hear it in your own words."

Rex mixed them drinks, which they carried to the sunshine of the patio, and Katie retold the story that she had already repeated several times at the police station.

"There's a certain irony in the justice of it," she said. "Mary punishes Alexa for causing the death of her parents, then in return Alexa reaches from the grave to punish her. It's sort of a ripple effect."

"Were you frightened as you faced Mary?"

She hesitated, then answered honestly, her voice barely audible. "I was scared to death." It relieved her to admit it.

"I'm glad. You'd have been a fool not to have been scared."

"But I wanted to be brave."

"Brave people act in spite of their fear. You did that."

"Yes, I did, didn't I? And I feel great about that and about solving the case on my own. I've never felt so competent, but I can't help feeling sorry for Mary."

"Sorry for a murderer?"

"Yes. In spite of having everything Alexa's

money could provide, or perhaps *because* of having so much given to her, Mary grew up a disadvantaged child. She grew up thinking that everyone owed her something — something she wasn't getting. And nobody ever set her straight."

Rex rolled his eyes. "Next you'll be saying the murder really wasn't Mary's fault."

"Oh, it was her fault, all right." She shuddered as she thought about the police pictures of the murder scene. "But I still have some sympathy for her. Riches fell into her lap. It would have taken a strong person to refuse Alexa's gifts. Mary never had a chance to learn whether or not she could make it on her own."

"Maybe the state will give her a chance to develop a new career. Perhaps she'll have a true talent for making license plates."

"You're heartless."

Before he could reply, the telephone rang. He answered, then called her. "It's McCartel."

She took the phone. "Mac! It's over. Mary Bethel's in custody — and so is Elizabeth Wright."

"I heard. It's on every news station in South Florida. Are you okay? They said you were shot."

"Bullet just grazed my arm. I'm fine."

"Congratulations. You did a great job."

"It's a relief to have it behind me."

"Don't dream of relaxing. We have another assignment. A biggie."

She sighed. "Could you tell me about it tomorrow? I've had enough excitement for one day."

"Right. Talk to you tomorrow. Great job, Katie girl."

She replaced the receiver and joined Rex again at the pool. He had served the chowder, and they sat down to eat.

"You're a great cook, Katie."

"It was a case of have to." She grinned at him. "I was starving. Food has never tasted so good."

"Glad to hear it."

She savored the subtle flavorings of the chowder, bit into a buttered roll. When they finished eating she sighed and pushed her plate and bowl aside. "Mac says we have another job."

"That's what detectives do. They detect. Are you up for it?"

"The Chitting case has given me a lot to think about. I'd be lying if I said I didn't feel a pride of accomplishment, a new self-confidence. Someday I might even be brave enough to go back to classroom teaching, but for now, I think I belong right here in Key West at the McCartel/Hassworth agency."

"I'm glad. Very glad."

"How did things go for you in New York?"

"Great. Dad wants me to come home, take

over the hotel chain as he goes into retirement."

She looked across the pool at the privacy fence, refusing to meet his gaze. What would she do without him! "What did you tell him?"

"I told him no. I'm like you, Katie. I think I belong right here in Key West. I need the warmth of community support — especially of one person in this community."

"I'm glad. Really glad."

He rose and came to her side, pulling her to her feet as he took her in his arms. She made no protest.

About the Author

Award-winning author Dorothy Francis works in her home studios in Iowa and the Florida Keys. Her short mystery fiction has appeared in *Woman's World, Futures, Murderous Intent Mystery Magazine, HandHeldCrime,* Orchard Press Mysteries, as well as on thecase.com. Her short story "When in Rome," won a Derringer award in 1999. Her mysteries for young adults have won wide acclaim and can be found in most libraries in the country.

This is Dorothy's first adult mystery novel, a suspense thriller combining a first-rate puzzle with some wonderfully entertaining character portraits. She is currently at work on a second adult mystery novel.

The employees of Thorndike Press hope you have enjoyed this Large Print book. All our Thorndike and Wheeler Large Print titles are designed for easy reading, and all our books are made to last. Other Thorndike Press Large Print books are available at your library, through selected bookstores, or directly from us.

For information about titles, please call:

(800) 223-1244

or visit our Web site at:

www.gale.com/thorndike
www.gale.com/wheeler

To share your comments, please write:

Publisher
Thorndike Press
295 Kennedy Memorial Drive
Waterville, ME   04901